To Rachel, with
love,

Claribel Alegría
D J Flakoll

ASHES
OF
IZALCO

a novel by
Claribel Alegría
and
Darwin J. Flakoll

translated by
Darwin J. Flakoll

CURBSTONE PRESS

An original publication by Curbstone Press
printed in the U.S. by BookCrafters

Cover design by Bob Baldock

This publication was supported in part by donations from
individuals, and by grants from The National Endowment for the
Arts, Washington, DC, and The Connecticut Commission on the
Arts, a state arts agency whose funds are recommended by the
Governor and appropriated by the State Legislature.

ISBN: 0-915306-83-2 cloth
ISBN: 0-915306-84-0 paper
LC: 89-62125

Distributed to the trade by
The Talman Company
150 Fifth Avenue, New York, NY 10011

CURBSTONE PRESS • 321 JACKSON ST .• WILLIMANTIC, CT 06226

To our parents.

"Serán ceniza, mas tendrá sentido;
polvo serán, mas polvo enamorado."

— Francisco de Quevedo

ASHES OF IZALCO

Chapter One

The luncheon dishes clash and rattle in the kitchen. María grumbles to herself in a steady monotone, and Dad, strangely shrunken now, defenselessly old, lies asleep in the darkened bedroom. I've taken off my sandals, and the chocolate brown tiles are cool against my feet. The whitewashed arches march around the patio: circus elephants linked tail to trunk, enclosing the blaring bougainvillea, the file of rosebushes, the central fountain where Alfredo and I used to splash and scream, the shaded jasmine, the papaya tree, the star pine with its ivy-choked trunk.

It's hot, hot, hot. The leaves are motionless. A single humming bird flits, hangs suspended, darts to a golden cup, blends with the foliage, zooms off over the red-tiled roof. A damp towel of air presses against me: earthquake weather, Paul would say. Perhaps Izalco, ten kilometers to the south, is gathering itself for a mountainous belch as it did once before when I was seven. Frank mentions that in his diary. The wrinkled cloud glowed pink at night and dulled to dark red after each rumbling explosion. There was no sun during the day, and sulphurous flakes drifted down in an infernal snowfall that coated streets and roofs and the leaves of trees. People walked silently, handkerchiefs covering their noses, ashes deadening their footsteps. No. I'm still upset. The sky is hazy, and there'll be a thunderstorm this evening; that's all.

I should be writing letters, but there's plenty of time: I'll be here a month. Dad would be better off with us, but he doesn't want to leave his house, his town, his dead. He's too old to make a change, and Paul would start resenting him before the week was out, would grow silent and irritable, would weave pockets of tension in the air with nervous fingers. I would have to absorb his sullen outbursts behind the closed bedroom door, while Dad sat in the living room,

9

expecting it as his due to be waited on, entertained. Impossible! Besides, I tried last evening after dinner.

"If I leave Santa Ana," he said, "it will be for Nicaragua. If not, I'll just stay here."

He doesn't really see the house, or me, or the people who call. He looks past us into the shadowy corners, half expecting to surprise Death standing there.

Her bunch of keys at my waist. The moment of displacement this morning when he looked at me and forgot, slipped years back into the past. He thought I was she; he almost made a gesture, almost called me by her name before he recovered. For a dizzy second, yes, I was she, facing Papa Manuel years ago after Mama Carmen died, feeling the tiredness and emptiness in him. Time lurched back into its customary groove, and we looked away from each other, ashamed that identities are so fragile, so interchangeable. I hurried on down the corridor, her bunch of keys jingling against my hip, to supervise the cooking.

He shouldn't be alone. Perhaps Alfredo and Ana can come and live here. He wouldn't mind the children; he'd enjoy the noise, the questions, the responsibility for settling their quarrels.

One of these days I'll have to take him for a walk around town; I haven't done that for years. I want to climb the hill and look down at the dusty spiderweb of Santa Ana stretching across the valley, anchored to the coffee plantations surrounding it. I want to see it once more in the crystal morning after a night's rain, embossed on the green surface of El Salvador. I want to climb the hill at noon when white clouds swell large and float low over the houses, nuzzling the sleepy town where nobody has learned the tense, big-city stride, the staccato of metropolitan speech. I want to see the silver web at night, with lights glimmering along its threads like dewdrops.

Santa Ana is small. It stretches from the church of Santa Lucia, where the stolid virgin offers her eyes — two fried eggs on a platter — to idlers lounging in the park across the street,

10

and continues as far as the knotted, elephant-leg ceiba, whose branches are themselves horizontal trees shading the bright-skirted women selling *pupusas*. Its branches shelter the fortress gate where a sentry fights his immobile battle against sleep; they shade the colonel, hands behind his back, frowning down at his tenacious enemy: the dust which dulls his polished boots.

In the other direction, Santa Ana extends from the railway crossing (Stop! Look! Listen!) where the road from Chalchuapa carries oxcarts and barefoot peasants to market, through the business district to Don Jaime's modern coffee mill (Largest In The World!) and the five wedding-cake houses of Don Jaime and his sons.

It's been years since I paused to look at the town, Santa Lucia's fried-egg eyes, the sparkling cobweb from the hill; years since I listened to the morning cries of street vendors, roosters that crow at all hours of day or night, midday murmurs drifing over pastel walls, forlorn dogs baying at the sinking moon while the clock in the dark corridor chimes and pauses, chimes and pauses, chimes.

The market this morning (María padding along behind me with her basket) brought back the small, familiar world of childhood: mounds of nances and candies; odors of sweat, urine, tamarinds; live iguanas with malevolent red eyes, thick tongues, short, ugly legs strapped behind their backs. Nothing has changed: the same starving dogs with marimba ribs and bony tails tucked between their legs slink among the stands; potbellied, naked children dart like fish through the dust and garbage; beggars with open sores await alms and death along walls tattooed with filth, spittle, and peeling posters.

"Niña Carmen, I'm so sorry..." she goes on weighing out potatoes and platitudes. Strange that they recognize me, remember me after all this time: that I'm still Niña Carmen to all of them. We walk on, squeezing through the crowded aisles.

11

"María, we'll have to get some yucca! It's been years since I've had yucca and sausage." Forgive me, Mother! *Que Dios la tenga en su Gloria*...Stop it! Superstitions! Nuns gliding along the cold corridors of Asunción; catechism classes; the chapel with Padre Antonio bending over the pulpit, light catching on his glasses as he looks down, down, into my soul with round, empty eyes. Mamaita, still and cold in the dark. Putrefaction and worms! And Cucarachita Mandinga wails and cries. Stop it!

The stickpin with Neto's picture.

"Isabel! What have you done with my pin?"

"I haven't seen it, *viejo*. It must be in one of your other suits."

Confusion, scurrying servants, the house turned upside down. Dad's face flushed red, veins swelling in his neck. He's never wrong; he couldn't have lost it. No, somebody hid it to annoy him.

"How are the tomatoes today?"

"Niña Carmen! It's been years! Terrible about your mother! I couldn't believe it when I heard the news..."

"Yes. Yes. Thank you. Two pounds please."

"Cata always used to bring you, remember? Such a good woman, Doña Isabel! So kind to everyone. Not snooty like some people. And all the charity she thought nobody knew about. God bless her! There you are: the very best. Thirty five *centavos*, please."

And Cata came home with the stickpin two days later.

"What luck, Doctor! Hilda — you know, Cross-eyed Hilda — found it in the market yesterday. She said to me, 'This is the Doctor's baby, isn't it?' and she said, 'Yesterday, when I was sweeping up, and I knew he's the only one who wears a picture of his dead baby in a stickpin.'"

"You see, Isabel!" Triumphantly, "I knew I hadn't lost it. You thank Cross-Eyed Hilda for me, Cata. Tell her to come to my office this afternoon."

My appendicitis attack came just after Neto's funeral, and Dad drove me to San Salvador for X-rays: a long, twisting,

12

hurting journey, with me lying in the back seat holding an icebag on my stomach. We stopped at the stone cutter's on the way back, and Dad told Don Enrique:

"That's the one. I want it to say: 'Ernesto Rojas Valdés. Born Santa Ana 10 October 1930. Died 19 January 1931.' "

The Ford jumped and jolted over the dirt road. I lay thinking about Neto's funeral, looking at Dad's neck, wondering with terror and curiosity about the fat, red worm of my swollen appendix inside me.

"I hope you won't have to go back and buy another stone for me."

"Idiot!" he growled, and he didn't say another word all the way home. But he carried me into bed and refilled the icebag himself. He put it on my stomach and mussed my hair before he went out to make his afternoon calls.

Did Neto's death have anything to do with it? Can you point to any one event and say: here it is; this is the pebble that lost its grip and started the avalanche? Dates mean nothing in Santa Ana. A single lightening and darkening of the small, hot stage is meaningless; it is needless to assign names and numbers to the alternation of days and nights. In Santa Ana events are remembered by their proximity to the milestones of birth, marriage, and death. But why did he have to die? I shiver, twist uneasily in my chair as I always do when the *why* of death confronts me. I'm in the patio before Neto was born, with Mother calling from the bedroom:

"Get into your white dress, Carmen. We have to leave right away."

We walk along the street, Mother holding my hand.

"Don't be afraid," she tells me. "You'll see how beautiful Margarita is going to be: all covered with flowers and with her eyes closed, just as if she's asleep. That's all death is, really," she smiles down at me, "just a deep sleep."

The house is crowded, the air thick with a buzz of voices and an odor of lilies. Carlitos sees us enter and comes over.

"Do you want to see her?" he asks. Mother pushes me toward him and goes into the bedroom to be with Doña

13

Josefina. There are more murmuring people in the living room, but I see only her: lying there in a white dress like mine, hands clasped on her breast, suspended by candlelight in the semi-darkness.

"Do you want to touch her?" Carlitos asks. "She's cold."

Her dark curls stand out against the satin pillow. Her eyes aren't closed; they are half open. She is as still as a doll in a cellophane box.

"Don't be afraid of her," Niña Leti says severely. Everyone in the room looks at me.

"Go ahead, touch her. She's a little angel now."

Carlitos pushes me toward the box, raises my hand and places it on Margarita's cheek. She is as cold as a windowpane. I can't speak or breathe.

Don Carlos and the two uncles walk into the room. All three are wearing dark glasses. The murmuring stops. Don Carlos looks at her, bends down to kiss her cold forehead, and slowly closes the lid.

It isn't just a deep sleep; she's a cold thing in a closed box. She wasn't pretty; her lips were all blue. My joints dissolve, and there is a vulnerable emptiness between my chest and my legs. Carlitos reaches for me.

"Do you want to come to the cemetery with us? There's room in our car." I shake my head as hard as I can.

Doña Josefina appears in the doorway between Mother and another lady. She screams and stretches her arms toward the closed box. I squeeze past her, squirm through the grownups in the vestibule and out the front door where another crowd is waiting to see them carry the box out. I curl up in our car, which smells of lilies for dead people, and I close my eyes tight, tight, tight.

I have so many memories of Mother. I remember her dressed in black for funerals, wearing a hat and veil for a wedding, in a two-piece suit for her trips to San Salvador. But after reading Frank's diary I am confused, disoriented, as if I had never really known her after all. I need to order my memories, trace each feature and characteristic, rescue her

14

from chaos and oblivion. Now, sitting in her chair in the patio, among her flowers and birds, I have to review what is left of her, fend off the feeling that she has become a complete stranger. Here, beside her potted begonia, she seems less dead. It's hard to think of that — not just her death, but the sudden sensation that I never really knew her, that I only used her as a mirror. All those years at her side, and I never guessed. Some line in her face, some fugitive expression, would have provided the clue, had I paused to look for it. How stupid! Always talking of me, me, me. She would listen and smile, and she would say:

"Yes, *hijita*, of course..." and go on watering her plants, keys jingling as she moved, retaining behind her eyes a store of memories that she concealed from us all.

"Hurry, Carmen!" she says. "Lola will be waiting for us." I get bored at Lola's. There are no books, and Alicia only chatters about dresses and parties, about her friends who, she always reminds me, are the richest girls in San Salvador. Mother is bored by Lola too, but it's a way of escaping Santa Ana for a while.

My clearest memories are of her making preparations for those escapes: visits to Lola or Maruca in San Salvador, infrequent trips to Guatemala or Mexico on the pretext of visiting relatives she really didn't care about. She makes no pretense of hiding her excitement as she rifles through drawers, lays articles of clothing out on the bed. Bells ring in her voice, and Dad stands by, vaguely troubled, twirling his golden keychain around a forefinger.

When she returned from one of her trips, her suitcases were always crammed with books: French and English novels, metaphysical texts which unveiled Rosicrucian mysteries, books of poetry. At night, while Dad sat in the corner, inundated in the blare and crackle of shortwave news from Nicaragua, Mother read her books. An invisible wall cut her off from us, from Dad, from the old house itself. She read them page by page, rationing her small daily escapes drop by drop, like a shipwreck victim on a lifeboat.

15

It wasn't that she had an incessant urge to travel, a yearning to forever be someplace else: she wasn't that kind of person. Remembering her, I have the sensation of someone carrying a heavy burden except when she was away from home or hidden behind a book. That burden could only have been my father.

I'll have to remind Cata to take care of the plants or they'll wither now that Mother's gone. Dad, the plants: how many other things? What things would shrivel and dry if I were to disappear suddenly? Our plants wouldn't: Paul waters them when he comes home from the office. Does he miss me? I imagine him putting the car in the garage, methodically changing clothes, poking and digging at his roses and tomatoes until dark, eating dinner quietly while the children chatter about their day at school.

Frank noticed Mother's quiet sadness; I have only become aware of it now. I was young, of course, absorbed with myself, swept with curiosity and misgivings by the mystery of love. But Santa Ana started shrinking for me before I was seventeen, and I began to feel the gray weight of it, the irritating, fenced-in feeling that radiates from the cobbled streets and unbroken walls of the house fronts, the tepid, somnolent monotony of it. What would I have become if I had been forced to live here, as she did, until the end?

Mother didn't even go marketing; Cata took care of that. After breakfast you tell the cook what to prepare for lunch, you inspect the bedrooms and the tiled floors, water the plants in the main patio and perhaps pull a few weeds in the flower beds. Then comes a long, empty stretch which you can fill by reading or writing letters, or just sitting if it's too hot. The children come home for lunch at noon, and time passes rapidly until they're off again. You welcome the oblivion of the siesta hour until 3, when it's time for iced refreshments. After that, Dad would go out to make his afternoon calls, and Mother would read or listen to records. We children would come home from school at 5, just about the time visitors started dropping by. An interminable stream of relatives; they came to chew over the same morsel of gossip; they chew on it, savor it, chew it again and again until a tastier bit appears.

Señorita Soto never married. She is the sphinx of Santa Ana. Her window-framed immobility poses a question that I didn't understand for many years. Nobody knows what really happened. Some say it was a married man, others say he was a Turk. The fact is that no young man ever came calling after that. When I was little I assumed, whenever I saw her leaning over her balcony like a spider in the center of her dusty web, that she was simply growing older without ever getting married, without forming her own family like everyone else.

Years ago, when I returned for the first time, I saw her sitting there. Afterwards, whenever I came with Paul and the children, and now just two days ago. Each time older and more shrivelled. A spider that never trapped anything, huddled in the center of the web. Sitting behind the grille every day, not reading, not knitting, looking out over the same street where the same dust arises behind each automobile and returns to its same spot. An entire lifetime of stolid bitterness and public resignation.

Señorita Soto's immobility is a challenge to the city, a mockery of the insensate bustling of passersby who believe that something is happening in Santa Ana. Nothing happens. Señorita Soto has been on the lookout, but she has waited in vain and finally metamorphosed into a public monument.

Dad listened to shortwave broadcasts at night, while Mother sat in that chair at the opposite end of the corridor reading French novels. The bookcase is filled with volumes which only she ever opened. She dreamed of Paris all her life and painstakingly taught me French in hopes I would one day study at the Sorbonne. But she never saw Paris.

Dad visited Paris when I was very young. He came back with hundreds of postcards, anecdotes, a red fire engine for Alfredo, and a doll for me that I named María Julia. For years after his trip, he and Papa Manuel exchanged reminiscences about the city, recalling restaurants, certain street corners, the chestnut trees along the banks of the Seine. There were gaps in Dad's chronicles. Sometimes, telling men friends about the trip, his voice would drop to a murmur, and suddenly all of them would burst out laughing. Mother, sitting across the room with the women, would turn to furious stone whenever that happened, but I was the only one who noticed.

I learned later that there are many Parises. Papa Manuel's centered around the School of Medicine, spread through Montparnasse as far as the Bois de Boulogne, was filled with gas-lit restaurants, velvet-lined cabarets and elegant young ladies who were accessible to a rich Central American student. Papa Manuel studied under Charcot and knew Freud. Whenever someone mentioned Salvadorean intellectuals admiringly, he would purse his lips and blow explosively through his mustache.

"This house," his voice is soft, reflective, "is one of the oldest in Santa Ana. It was bigger when I was a boy. In those days, with outbuildings and stables, it covered the whole block."

He points a shaky forefinger toward the patio.

"Aunt Luisa had her hammock between those two posts. I remember her lying there rolling little cigars out of tobacco leaves, or polishing the silver coins she kept in bags. She would spread them out on wooden trays and leave them in the sun all afternoon."

Papa Manuel never complained about poverty. After Mama Carmen died, he lived alone in the old house with his memories, his pictures of her and Paris, his thick, dusty books illustrated by Gustave Doré. As far back as I can remember he ate dinner and slept at our house. In the morning when Alfredo and I were leaving for school, he would step jauntily off toward his own home and dim library, flourishing his ebony cane. He spent his days translating Buffón, snorting at the latest outrages of the perfidious English, dashing breakneck to the window whenever a pretty girl passed by.

18

Dad's Paris centered on the Eiffel tower and swept from the Champs Elysee to the Folies Bergiere and Place Pigalle. He visited the Louvre, though, and made a point of seeing La Gioconda, the Venus de Milo, and the Winged Victory of Samothrace. Whenever he saw a chance, he would slip these into the conversation to show Mother he had not completely ignored the world of culture. If Mother was feeling put out with him, she would sniff, toss her head, and say icily:

"For every minute you spent in the Louvre, you spent hours inspecting garters and silk stockings at the Moulin Rouge."

Once a week, despite my protests and feigned stomach aches, Mother propelled me to *Asunción* where she and Madre Merci would converse in French about classical literature and European history. Madre Merci was tiny and desiccated. Over the years her small frame had become bent under the weight of God's love and her heavy purple habit.

The three of us sit in a small, barren room which smells of candlewax and mouse droppings. The chairs have high, straight backs and are covered with bristly red velvet that prickles the underside of my legs. My feet dangle above the floor, and I'm not permitted to tuck them under me or to scratch in Madre Merci's presence. I can't even slip off into my own dream world, because Mother will ask me to review the entire conversation when we get home. From time to time, Madre Merci directs a question to me, pushing her face so close to mine that her veil tickles my nose and her decayed breath suffocates me. Uncomprehendingly, I endure royal geneologies and rambling accounts of kingly treachery.

Mother's Paris, learned from her books, from Papa Manuel and Madre Merci, was peopled by Robespierre, Marie Antoinette, Victor Hugo, Lamartine, Balzac, and the Impressionists: a Paris of phantoms gliding about the Palais Royale, domiciled in the Pantheon; an enchanted city of daring brush strokes and pastel pigments; an evanescent web of chiaroscuro and words.

Such visions were too subtle for Dad's tastes. He read the daily newspaper and, with the help of a dictionary, puzzled

19

out the English texts in the *National Geographic*. He dreamed, not of Paris, but of returning to the strong brown and green landscape of Nicaragua.

"No one bothered to make sure I got an education," he tells us, fixing his eyes on Alfredo. "The only one who helped me was Uncle Gregorio."

"Nonsense, Alfonso," Mother interrupts. "That old man was mean to you."

"No, Isabel, don't be unfair. He taught me to be a man." Dad rubs the side of his nose and focusses on some faraway point in space.

"I remember when I was nine years old, my brothers and I were walking around the ranch one day when we saw a cow giving birth to a calf. We helped her as best we could, and I felt happy looking at that little brown and white calf with its wet, curly hair. I thought what a wonderful thing it was to help bring life into this world, and I made up my mind right then to become a doctor and an obstetrician."

Dad shakes his head and frowns down at Alfredo and myself sitting at his feet.

"My brothers laughed when I told them.

"'What do you mean, study?' they said. 'You're going to stay here and work on the ranch like the rest of us.'

"But I convinced my Dad to let me go to Uncle Gregorio's. He was a photographer in the town of León where there was a school.

"'You?' my uncle said. 'What are you doing around here?'

"'I want to go to school, Uncle. If you'll let me stay with you, maybe I can help you somehow.'

"He thought about it for a while.

"'All right,' he said finally, 'you can sleep in the darkroom, and you can clean the studio and run errands for me.'

"Uncle Gregorio lived alone and had a terrible temper," Dad grins as he recalls those days. "He made me read the newspaper aloud during his siesta, and every time I made a mistake he'd give me a clip on the ear. Sometimes when he was in a good mood, he'd take me riding on his mule. He would

20

tell stories about his life and repeat over and over that I should study hard and always be honorable and help drive the Yankees out of Nicaragua when I grew up.

"But there were other days when he'd get up on the wrong side of bed, and then, God help me!

"'I'm beating you to make a man of you,' he would say. 'Some day you'll be grateful to me.'"

Dad nods reprovingly at Mother, who is concentrating on her sewing.

"When I brought her to Nicaragua, I had an awful time convincing her we should even call on Uncle Gregorio."

"It was because he had made you suffer so, *viejo*. I still don't see how you can forgive him all that."

"When I did introduce my beautiful wife and show him my parchment degree, you should have seen him! As happy as a boy! He felt he'd earned the degree himself by beating knowledge into my thick skull.

"No." Dad gazes sternly at Alfredo once more. "I owe Uncle Gregorio a lot. He bought me my first pair of shoes, and he taught me to be a man."

Dad and Mother: two opposed temperaments. Mother was the shrub clinging to the edge of the precipice, bending gracefully to the wind's buffeting; Dad, the granite boulder shouldering out of the water, reveling in his unflinching resistance to the waves. This is the image I have of the two of them.

But they didn't react that way when Neto died. Dad was crushed by the fact that all his skill and knowledge wasn't enough to save his own son's life. After the funeral, he referred his patients to another doctor and sat in the corridor for hours each day. Mother, though, didn't even cry at the funeral. She carried on with her household affairs as usual, receiving visitors and condolences quietly, while Dad ignored people, conversations, and everything that went on around him.

21

It took my appendectomy to bring Dad back to normal, but it was Mother who sat all night with me in the hospital room after the operation. I lay awake that first night, my mouth bitter with vomit, my mind conjuring up pitchers of ice water, astringent tamarind juice, lemonade. I saw the jet of the patio fountain splashing into the clear pool. Alfredo and I, naked to the waist, danced under gurgling gutters while a cloudburst drenched us and water ran in streams from the ends of my hair. I pretended to be asleep, but peered from under my lashes until Mother, her figure illuminated by a single bar of light from the corridor, leaned her head back against the wall and closed her eyes. When I was sure she was asleep, I undid the cap of the icebag, fished out pieces of ice, and sucked them.

Some water must have wet my bandage; two days later the wound was angry red and I was delirious. Mother nursed me through the fever and my slow convalescence. I remember her arm under my head while I drank water or a few spoonfuls of soup. I remember her bathing me with a soapy cloth, massaging my back and legs with lavender lotion.

The day I took my first steps Mother retired to her room and went to bed. She wouldn't speak to anyone except to say she had a headache and wasn't hungry. The Shrub had lost its will to hold fast to the cliff.

I lived with the two of them, loved and accepted them with never a second thought: they were simply my parents. Now I can see them as individuals, each with his own potentialities, desires, limitations, and each with a handful of days loaned him against a final accounting. That is my own case as well.

Chapter Two

"Niña Carmen," Cata startles me. "Niña María Luisa is at the door."

But she isn't; she has bustled through the vestibule on Cata's heels and is on top of me with her quick, nervous embrace, kissing my hair and cheek with the voracity of a chicken pecking at grains of corn.

"Ay, you're looking more like your poor mother every day!" She plumps down in the other chair. "What a terrible thing! Who could have guessed it? Isabel looked so well! That's life! It was written; it had to happen. And she could have been saved if only they'd recognized it earlier. Strange the Doctor didn't realize what it was. Your poor Dad! It's good that he's resting. I just can't imagine him without Isabel; they were so united. You don't see marriages like that any more, and not many funerals as well-attended as your Mother's. The procession was seven blocks long; I counted. Why, this very morning I was at Niña Fina's and she was telling me..."

"Look, Carmen," Mother tells me, "that's the bell that Mamita María's grandparents donated. They had it brought over from Spain." We enter the church. Mother and Alfredo cross themselves; Dad strides on ahead.

"Here they are," he says in a loud voice. Mother hushes him and goes to where he is standing beside the main altar. She bends forward to look at the floor. We are all quiet as she deciphers the blurred, archaic inscription cut into the stone:

"Francisco Silva, born in the Canary Islands 7 April 1691. Died in the arms of the Holy Mother Church, Santa Ana, 5 October 1754. Clara Martínez de Silva, born in Metapán, 10

May 1700. Died in the arms of the Holy Mother Church, Santa Ana, 11 August 1762."

We had lunch at María Luisa's that day.

"Come with me; I want to show you something." María Luisa pulls me by the arm to her bedroom, her eyes glinting with malice. "See that? You can still make out the marks. This was your great-great-grandmother's bedroom, and that was the famous secret door that led to Papa Jorge's store. Your mother has told you the story, hasn't she?"

I lie, saying yes, some of it. María Luisa continues enthusiastically.

"Ah, Papa Jorge was a scoundrel! Mama Juana was left a widow while she was still young and beautiful, and Papa Jorge kept after her and kept after her until he gave her a baby. Mamita María and Lupe, her sister, were studying at a nun's school in Guatemala, and they didn't know anything about it, of course. Mamita María was only fifteen at the time. Nobody in town knew anything about it, because Mama Juana never left the house. Then do you know what happened?"

María Luisa watches my face, certain now that I know none of the story.

"When Mama Juana's two girls came home at the end of the school year, Papa Jorge took a fancy to Mamita María, who was a real beauty. He married her within two months.

"Poor Mama Juana never said a word to her daughters or to anybody. The two girls thought the baby boy belonged to one of the servants and that Mama Juana had adopted him."

"How did anyone ever find out?" I ask.

"Mamita María didn't know until much, much later. But one of the servants finally told Lupe about it, and Lupe came running to Mamita María with the story. That Lupe was bad — jealous because Mamita María was more beautiful."

"What was Papa Jorge like?"

She raises her skinny, scarecrow arms over her head.

"A prince!" she closes her eyes ecstatically. "What a way he had with the girls! He was already an old man when I was just a tiny thing, but he was still handsome and still a devil.

He was forty when he married Mamita María, and she hadn't yet put away her dolls. She didn't understand why Papa Jorge would spit on the floor and walk out of the room whenever her mother came to visit her."

"Have you visited your great-aunts?" I start as her voice reaches me. "Ah, they're worse than I am. Bumps on a log. They didn't even go to the funeral, did they? No, they never go anywhere, not even to Mass..."

The dark, damp house. Blind Virginia seated in the cane rocking chair, creaking away the days, months, years. In Aunt Ginny's shrivelled mind there is scarcely room for the ups and downs of her emotional entanglement with her cats; a deeply-grooved memory of her aborted, turn-of-the-century romance with Sebastian Molina, and a few fragments of sociability when she pretends to recognize one or another great-great-nephew that her milk-white eyes have never seen.

There's no place for maiden aunts in Santa Ana. Perhaps things are different now, but twenty years ago the only future for a "society" girl lay in marrying anyone who was remotely acceptable. To work for a living was unthinkable — a dishonor to the family name — and spinsters were only permitted to make candy for their nephews and nieces and to crochet doilies. They would send the candy around to us a few days before the end of the month: a reminder to our parents that their rent was coming due. The doilies were birthday gifts to their married sisters. Those in the worst circumstances would bake cookies furtively and send the cook around the neighborhood to sell them as if they were her own.

No wonder Mother felt stifled in this town. There is not one theatre or concert hall, not a single restaurant, not even a decent cafe. There are no bookstores which offer anything besides detective and love stories and children's textbooks.

25

The men of Santa Ana's society, of course, have the Casino, with its garish black rafters and egg-yellow walls. The architect tried to imitate a Spanish hostel, but he neglected to stain the walls with century-old soot, to lower the high, tropical ceiling to create an intimate atmosphere.

It's the cocktail hour, and members begin to drift in from their country mansions, bank offices, legal suites. The tables, empty at three p.m., become animated. Snatches of wilted conversation drift through the semi-darkness. Ancient waiters, white jackets setting off mahogany skins, glide across the floor with trays of drinks.

Don Joaquín (3,600 acres and 100,000 *quintales* of coffee) is at his table. It isn't really his table, but no one sits there without his invitation. He's playing "horses" with Don Miguel. He shakes the leather cup; the dice rattle hollowly and spill out on the table. Neither of them is interested in the game, but it's a way of passing time without having to make conversation.

Raúl Hernández (250 acres and 6,000 *quintales*) comes out of the treasurer's office where he has spent the last two hours checking the books. Several whiskies have helped ease his task, and he sways slightly, blinking into the gloom. He moves among the tables, glass in hand, slapping backs and greeting fellow members stridently. He stops at Don Joaquín's table and his manner changes. He clears his throat hesitantly and rocks back and forth on his heels, waiting as he has for years to be recognized, accepted, invited to draw up a chair. Don Joaquín ignores him and shakes the dice cup again.

"María Luisa, do you remember Frank Wolff?"

"How could I forget him? He was the Communist who came here pretending he was writing a novel, the liar! He came on orders from Moscow. He and Martí were the ones who planned the whole thing. Only God knows what might have happened if Martínez hadn't been president, but he knew what to do, all right..."

26

"What did he look like?"

"Let's see. He was tall, with brown hair and mean blue eyes. He had a long nose too; I'll bet he was a Jew."

She glances at her watch and jumps to her feet.

"Heavens! It's three o'clock, and I have to be at church. Now don't forget to say hello to the Doctor for me. I'll drop by again one of these days and we'll have a nice, long chat."

Washington is larger than Santa Ana. It has theatres, parks, museums, but life there seems just as restricted as Mother's was here. I'm tied to the house — making beds, vacuuming, cooking, doing dishes — more than she ever was with servants to do all the work. Life is lonely in the States. We live in the suburbs, go to the movies once a week, and once in a long, long time to the theatre. Apart from trips to El Salvador and to California to visit Paul's parents, we've never travelled. When we go on vacation or do anything outside our normal routine, Paul plans it like a military operation. He enjoys that more than doing the thing itself.

Ah, Paul, there's nothing spontaneous about you, my monosyllabic friend, dutiful husband, unimaginative helpmeet — not even when you make love. Fridays, Sundays and Tuesdays, unless the office workload has worn you down by Tuesday. Yes, my darling, my fuzzy, fumbling sweet. I'm married to the perfect Organization Man. And what remedy is there for that?

Chapter Three

"Hi!" Alfredo walks into the patio. "Where's Dad? Isn't he awake yet? He told me to be here before four."

He slumps into the chair María Luisa has just vacated.

"They say Colonel Gutiérrez won't last the night. The National Guard is making arrangements to bring the coffin there for the wake, so you won't get much sleep tonight. What a tough old buzzard! Spent a whole week dying. Remember the time Dad had a run-in with him when we were kids?"

We were playing by a bedroom window when two Guards brought a peasant to the barracks gate just in front of our house. His hands were tied behind his back by a cord bound around his paired thumbs: Salvadorean handcuffs. He stood with his head bowed, gazing sullenly at his bare feet. Colonel Gutiérrez strode out and spoke to him, but he didn't look up. The colonel spoke again harshly. The man answered with a single word. The colonel's fist lashed out, and the other staggered backward with blood gushing from his nose. The colonel stepped forward, fist drawn, and spoke sharply once more. It was then that Dad burst out the front door of our house, white smock flapping around his legs, his face flushed as it always gets when he's furious.

"That's a coward's trick!" he shouted. "you don't hit a man whose hands are tied!"

Colonel Gutiérrez reddened and glowered at the two Guards.

"You tend to your patients, Doctor," he replied curtly, "and I'll take care of law and order in this town."

Dad looked squarely at him.

"If you hit that man again, I am going to telephone General Solórzano to complain about your conduct."

28

The Colonel's jaw muscles knotted; he abruptly motioned the two Guards to take the prisoner away. The man, his shirt front bright with blood, disappeared behind the gates. Dad and the Colonel exchanged a few more sentences in lower tones. We couldn't hear what they were saying, but when Dad wheeled and stalked back across the street, his face was still an angry red. Colonel Gutiérrez looked up and down the street to see if anybody had been watching before he, too, turned and went into the barracks.

"I remember," I answer. "Dad won, as usual."

"'Jalisco never loses,'" Alfredo quotes and shakes his head admiringly.

"Do you remember Frank Wolff, Alfredo?"

"A little. Why?"

"Nothing in particular. He wasn't a Communist, was he?"

Alfredo snorts.

"That's a wild yarn the old women around here scare themselves with. He was just a harmless drunk like me. Remember the Christmas he spent with us? He gave me a big tow truck and a whole bunch of firecrackers, and I burnt your dress and nearly got a licking."

He squints at the ceiling, gnaws his lower lip.

"He used to come here an awful lot to play chess with Dad, and he was nice to both of us. Once he took me to see a Tom Mix or a Tim McCoy picture."

"Do you remember what he looked like?"

"Let's see. He was tall and sort of skinny. He stooped a little when he walked. And he had pale blue eyes."

Alfredo stands up suddenly.

"Looks like Dad is never going to wake up, and I have to run some errands for Ana. Tell him I'll be back."

Alfredo remembers him better than I do. Frank gave me a doll that Christmas. I hadn't yet decided to become a poet.

29

That came later when I was about nine. I scribbled verses in ruled notebooks and showed them to Mother, Augusto, Don Lino, to anybody who took the least interest or was too polite to say no. Mother encouraged me, and Augusto or Don Lino would trudge through my scrawlings, nodding politely, to please her. Sometimes in the evening, Mother would call me to her bedroom and read me poems of St. John of the Cross, St. Therese, Fray Luis de León.

But Don Chico made an agnostic and Philistine out of me and convinced me that science was the only worthwhile pursuit. He taught biology and botany in Hectór's school: a tiny, dark Indian who interspersed his lectures with old legends or the indignant outbursts of a 19th century reformer; an intense, slightly absurd little bundle of a man who used a mixture of lard and lemon juice on his straight, black hair to keep it from falling over his eyes.

"In Ataco," he tells us, "the Devil's oxcart rolls through the streets at midnight: an old, faded cart hauled by invisible oxen. It rumbles through the dark streets at full speed, and inside it rides a man, also invisible, who screams and screams and screams..."

Or again:

"In Ataco," he tells us, "there is one school with classes running through the fourth grade. Children of eight have to drop out of school during the harvest to help their parents pick coffee. They get paid by the sack, just like the grownups, but they aren't given any food. The owners say they don't work fast enough. Their mothers and fathers have to make enough food for two people stretch to feed six or eight. How can children who are fed like that find the strength to study? No!" his voice trembles with conviction, "this country can never be great until its children get enough to eat and its people build fewer *cantinas* and more classrooms."

"Doesn't it worry you to have Carmen go to Hectór's school?" Celia's edged voice inquires of Mother. "Of course

30

Héctor himself is wonderful, but all the other teachers are Communists like that Don Chico Luarca. And the friends she makes there! Why, hardly any of them are from good families. Hectór even lets Turks in..."

Chapter Four

Isn't Alfredo here yet? Dad asks grumpily, combing his hair back with his fingers. "I told him to be here by four."

He sinks heavily into the chair opposite me.

"I don't know what to do, Carmen. He's irresponsible, cut from the same cloth as your mother's brothers. He'd be late to his own funeral."

"Now, Dad," I soothe him, "he came by a little while ago, but you were asleep. He said he'd be back soon."

"Why couldn't he wait until I woke up?" he grumbles. "I tell you, he's a calamity."

Despite myself, I slip into Mother's role of mediator. "He's behaved himself since I've been here. He hasn't been drinking at all."

Dad snorts.

"You know why, don't you? He got the scare of his life three months ago when he started urinating blood. His kidneys can't handle alcohol. But I know him. As soon as he thinks he can get away with it, he'll start in again. No more will power than a monkey.

"And how does he spend his time? He doesn't put in ten honest hours a week on the plantation. The rest of the time he runs around the country burning up gasoline. Gasoline and Liquor! What a way to squander the little we have! And he complains that I don't let him make decisions. If I did, we'd all be in the poorhouse right now."

His head moves slowly, ponderously, from side to side, his lower lip juts out reprovingly.

"I don't know, Carmen. I've tried to drill character into that boy, but I never got any help from your mother. I wanted him to have a profession, but he flunked out of college, what with all his chasing around and drinking."

32

He takes out his pipe, fills it with tobacco, lights it carefully and evenly, and squints through the blue clouds rising around his head.

"'Tell me who you run with, and I'll tell you who you are.' He learned to drink in the United States. I shouldn't have sent him. He came back with the vice and without the profession. I didn't want to send either of you; it was your mother's idea. And she was always taking his side. Well," he moves his free hand helplessly, "I've done what I can for him."

"What place did they give you?" I ask smugly. "Why aren't you first in your class like I am?"

"Look at your sister!" Dad shouts at him, waving his report card. "Aren't you ashamed of yourself? You should have been the girl of the family."

Dad peers at the clock in the corridor.

"Four o'clock. Time for the news from Nicaragua." He gets up painfully. "Do you want to listen to it?"

"You go ahead, Dad. I have to see how María is getting on with the dinner. Don't forget, there'll be six of us tonight."

"Know what?" Alfredo grins as we walk home from school. "Today I wound up at the tail end of the class, and from now on nobody's going to take that place away from me."

"You prefer Alfredo to me," I accuse mother hotly.

"No, Carmen," she answers gently, "it isn't that. Alfredo's different; he needs me more, that's all. You're stronger; you inherited Alfonso's character."

I look in on María, who needs no help from me, and I go to my room. I open the second drawer and take out Frank's diary

33

once more. There are things I still don't understand after reading it last night. The picture he paints of Mother is so different, so strange...

October 31, November 2, no, About mid-November, I think.

Chapter Five

November 16, 1931

I was sitting up for the first time today, working out an endgame on Virgil's chess set, when the doctor came in. He placed his bag on the table and, after greeting me, studied the board. White had three pawns and a knight, while black had two pawns, a bishop, and a slightly better position.

"Whose move?" he asked.

"White's."

He nodded, drew up a chair, and announced:

"White to win in twelve moves."

White did win within ten minutes and in exactly twelve moves, and I protested that he was taking advantage of an invalid. He laughed good-naturedly and at the same time stripped the tape off my abdomen with a single, excruciating wrench. The scar was neat, and there was only a little residual inflammation along the lip of the wound.

"That looks very good," he announced. "You can start walking around a bit this afternoon."

I asked him when I could travel and told him of my plans to visit Copan in Honduras and other Mayan ruins in Guatemala.

"Are you an archaeologist?" he asked.

"No, I'm a writer," I lied to simplify matters. "But I'm interested in the Mayan civilization, and I'd like to see as much of Central America as I can. I'm thinking of using it as background in a novel."

This second fib in three sentences slipped out without any intention on my part. I suppose I felt a compulsion to provide him with some acceptable reason for my presence here, some geographical justification, at least, for getting mixed up in a knife fight beside a pigsty.

He pursed his lips and prodded my abdomen around the wound. It was sore.

35

"That's a hard trip," he warned me. "You'll have to travel by horseback most of the way. I'd say you had better wait at least two weeks more."

I must have grimaced, because he laughed.

"I suppose Santa Ana seems small and dull to you."

"Frankly," I told him, "I can't imagine what I'll do with myself for the next two weeks."

"Well," he replied, "as a start, why don't you come to my house for dinner tonight. We'll play some chess, and I'll show you my Mayan collection."

It was an openhanded, unpremeditated gesture of hospitality. I'm susceptible to any offer of human warmth these days, and I accepted immediately.

After he left, I got up, dressed, and made a slow trip around the block to try out my legs. They seem to work normally, though I can't stand erect yet without the sensation that I'm split across the middle. I felt dizzy and weak after the walk, so I'm sitting here now, waiting for Virgil to return from a visit to his second congregation in Chalchuapa.

The more I see of Virgil, the less I understand him. He has an unwavering internal compass of some sort that's alien to my way of being. He has buried himself in this small, hot corner of nowhere for five years now, administering medicine to pigs, cattle and horses, and the word of God to his brown-skinned flock, with an intensity which is not so much self-sacrifice, I think, as it is a complete dismissal or negation of himself as an individual.

When I left home, for God's sake!, I headed for the biggest, gaudiest city I could think of, and started yammering for the world's attention at the top of my voice. Virgil came down here to erase himself, and I'm sure he's been forgotten by everyone except his immediate family back in the States.

His congregation? I have the feeling that their approval or adulation, or whatever it is they feel for him, is probably as unimportant in his scheme of things as is the hatred of the Catholics. I think he sees all of them as abstract victims of ignorance and error rather than as living human beings.

36

What does he think of me? Despite our long friendship, I'm sure it doesn't make the slightest difference to him whether I approve or disapprove, applaud or jeer, his chosen way of life.

I can't decide whether he changed in some basic way following that long-ago trip to the Sierras, or if, perhaps, the seed of what he was to become had not yet sprouted and put forth identifiable leaves. The Virgil I encountered a week ago was a complete stranger. Five minutes after my surprise arrival we had run out of hearty exclamations, the queries about "Whatever happened to old so-and-so?" and we were reduced to silence, punctuated by embarrassed snorts of laughter as each of us rummaged for something, anything, to say. We recognized in that short interval that we were irrevocably strangers.

It was he who finally found the first phrase after that uncomfortable pause:

"This is really great, Frank!" he enthused with all the innocent, showy falsity of a Woolworth diamond. "I haven't talked to anybody from home for going on five years."

That stopped me cold; I could find no ready answer. His mention of "home," his easy assumption that I considered Oregon my home, nailed down my perception of the chasm of unbridgeable years and wildly different experiences that lay between us. For an instant I grappled with the concept itself: the word "home" voiced in this exotic village to forge a link between two disparate strangers. I tried, in the silence that followed, to remember where I had mislaid mine, or whether I had ever really had one.

It certainly wasn't the house in Oregon, with the pedal organ wheezing hymns in the parlor and the granitic loom of my father dominating the domestic landscape like an unscaleable Matterhorn. Paris hadn't been a home either, any more than a sauna bath with its boiling-freezing alternations can be considered a home. And home was certainly not the bottle-strewn apartment in Hollywood.

No. My reunion with Virgil was uncomfortable, and the situation hasn't improved since then. I fell on him out of the blue, and before the week was out I lay flat on my back with my small intestine punctured, and he was nursing me as well as his pigs and congregation. Now I will be here two interminable weeks longer. But, knowing Virgil, I'm sure he will endure me with Christian fortitude as one additional cross he is destined to bear.

"Home" for me was to watch her coming along the corridor, pausing now and then, keys jingling, to straighten a chair or arrange a flower vase. It was my walks with her while I poured out my problems, my doubts, my enthusiasms. It was her presence, her special fragrance. And home was also Dad with his sayings, his aquiline profile, his doctor's satchel packed and squatting by the door.

November 17, 1931

Dinner at Dr. Rojas' last evening was more agreeable than I had anticipated. The combination of politics, good food, chess, and a literary discussion, was exhilarating, and I found myself reacting as a normal human being rather than a moral shell-shock case for the first time in months.

There was a difficult moment when I refused the wine, a fine St. Emilion which I'm sure was uncorked in my honor, but the others apparently took my refusal as an inexplicable *gringo* aberration — an overly-scrupulous observance of the Volstead Act, perhaps, or the effect of my association with that odd American missionary, Virgil Harris.

The men were talking politics when I arrived and, after the introductions were performed, I urged them to continue. Dr. Rojas' brother-in-law, Eduardo Valdés, is assistant manager of the Santa Ana newspaper, and he was citing the comings and goings of certain "barons" and military officials to sustain his thesis that a political crisis was brewing in the country. It gradually became clear that his "barons" were the small clique of immensely rich coffee planters who seem to control Salvadorean politics from behind the scenes.

"There's no hard proof, of course," he shrugged; "there never is until a conspiracy succeeds. But I'm willing to bet a month's salary that they're planning to overthrow Araujo."

"You may be right, " the Doctor agreed. "Don Jaime and the Colonel haven't been showing up at the Casino lately, and it would take something important to keep them away from their billiard game."

I was amused. The vision of generals, colonels and "barons" skulking about at night, laying plans to overthrow the government of this absurd little country, while the entire population followed and commented on their every move, seemed a delightful, comic opera touch.

"I'm sure they'll try it," Eduardo continued, "but this time they'll learn it isn't as simple as it used to be."

Don Manuel Valdés, Eduardo's father, was skeptical.

"What makes you think it won't be simple?" he asked.

"Because the peasants are behind the president for the first time," Eduardo answered emphatically. "Araujo has promised them land, and they won't permit him to be turned out of the palace like a discharged butler."

Don Manuel, a bird-like little man with a walrus mustache, sniffed.

"How are they going to oppose the military? They have no leaders, no organization, no weapons. An unarmed rabble can't stand up to trained soldiers. No, Eduardo, Araujo will go whenever two generals and a half dozen colonels decide they're tired of him.'

The younger man maintained an air of deference, but his voice took on a sharp edge.

"Don't forget it was an unarmed rabble that took the Bastille and stormed Versailles," he said. "It was barefoot peasants who made the Mexican revolution and factory workers who brought about the Bolshevik revolution. The

39

important question is whether or not a revolutionary situation exists, and it certainly does in this country."

Don Manuel gestured negligently.

"Your peasants are scattered about the countryside. They have no plans, no coordination. Why, they can't even read your newspaper to learn what's happening in the country. If by some miracle they were able to seize the capitol, they'd have to turn the government back into competent hands within a week. It takes a certain level of culture and education to manage any country, and your barefoot Bolsheviks are nowhere near that level."

Eduardo flushed.

"Our coffee barons and colonels aren't exactly noted for their cultural and intellectual attainments," he fired back, "but they've been running the country with no opposition ever since independence."

Mrs. Rojas laughed delightedly.

"*Touché,* Eduardo!" she entered the conversation for the first time. "You caught his weak side unguarded."

"El Salvador will be a malarial swamp peopled with half-alive, poverty-stricken illiterates until there is a real revolution and the country's wealth is put to work for all the people instead of for a handful," the young man declaimed.

I was watching Mrs. Rojas ply her crochet hook. She looked up, catching me in the act. To cover my adolescent surge of confusion, I asked her:

"What is your opinion about all of this, *Señora?*"

She bestowed on me one of those regal smiles with which lovely women acknowledge the surrender of yet another male.

"Women don't have the vote in El Salvador," she answered, "so when the men start arguing politics we merely close our ears and think our own, more important thoughts. One which occurs to me right now is that dinner must be ready."

She rose and led us into the dining room. I was seated on her right and disposed to strike up a conversation, but Eduardo

40

continued to hold the floor with his interminable, juvenile polemic.

Eduardo and his passion for politics!

"You must read the Communist Manifesto, Isabel," he points a peremptory finger at Mother. "You'll find practical Christianity there. Your beloved Tolstoy is a dithering old maid, but take Lenin now! You can feel the flame of truth in his writings. Capitalism is a decaying corpse," he flicks ashes scornfully on the tile floor, "and Lenin preached its funeral sermon years ago."

"Ay, Eduardo," Mother sighs and places an ash tray before him, "your Russian revolutionaries give me the shivers."

"Take a look around you," Eduardo demands. "Doesn't the misery in this country touch you? Have you ever so much as looked inside a *mesón* or a thatched hut in the countryside?"

"I know it's awful," she says, "but have you ever imagined what a revolution would be like? Those people are filled with hatred; they wouldn't stop chopping off heads until the country was running with blood."

"And who is responsible for that?" Eduardo flicks more ashes on the tiles. "Wouldn't you feel hatred too if you had been exploited, trampled on by the oligarchs, and treated like an animal all your life?"

The conversation turned to less controversial topics after the soup, and Mrs. Rojas abandoned her air of detached introspection to join in the talk. She seems a gay and charming person, but I had the feeling that in the presence of her husband and father she was restraining herself.

After coffee we adjourned to the patio, and Dr. Rojas beat me in a hard-won chess match. He employed a slashing, unorthodox attack which undermined my Queen's Indian defense and left my denuded king shivering in one corner of the

41

board to be annihilated by his rook, pawn and king. Don Manuel had retired, and Eduardo, who had been watching our play, challenged the Doctor. I ceded him my chair and strolled down the corridor to where Mrs. Rojas sat reading a book.

"Sit down, Mr. Wolff," she invited. "I hope you weren't bored by the overdose of local politics earlier this evening."

"Adam invented politics," I told her, "to annoy Eve and to give Cain and Abel something to quarrel about."

I picked up the book of poems she had been reading.

"Claudel! I saw his trilogy of plays in Paris a few years ago."

"You did?" Her eyes glowed and she leaned forward. "Tell me something about Paris, Mr. Wolff."

Yes, of course. That's what made the evening such a success. Shamelessly, I donned my Byronic, international adventurer's cloak and set out to charm and impress her, to watch her cup and savor my anecdotes of a Never-Never land inexpressibly remote from the languorous night of Santa Ana. We talked of Symbolist poetry, the Expressionists, and the newer wave of wild-eyed Surrealists. I was describing an evening at the Opera when a scraping of chairs announced that the chess game had ended.

November 19, 1931

The adhesions are bothering me, as the Doctor predicted they would, so I edged my way to his clinic this afternoon to ask for a painkiller. He gave me a sample bottle of pills and announced that from now on it was up to me to come back whenever I felt the need for a checkup or a late-afternoon game of chess. There was a small-boy eagerness in his expression when he brought up the subject of chess. I suspect Dr. Rojas finds the life of a small-town doctor too sedentary for his taste. He has the restless, impulsive manner of a man whose psychic motor is geared for another epoch, another mode of life: a knight errant, perhaps, following the

42

medieval tourney circuit in quest of the thrill of single combat rather than under the mystical spell of a Grail.

"We didn't get around to it the other evening," he changed the subject abruptly. "Would you like to see my Mayan relics now?"

I nodded, and let loose a window-rattling, "Isabel!"

Mrs. Rojas appeared in the doorway of his office wearing a reproving frown — she is clearly not a woman who relishes being shouted at — but her features relaxed into a smile when I greeted her.

"The keys to the Indian cabinet," the Doctor ordered. Mrs. Rojas hunted through the enormous bunch of keys at her waste, selected one, and led us into the dim vestibule. She opened a tall, glass-fronted cabinet, and the Doctor plunged into the shelves, loading my arms with fragile, pre-Columbian relics while I held my breath. We carried several dozen pieces to the patio and set them on the coffee table; fragile bowls and water vessels with geometric and animal designs painted in vegetable pigments, incense burners hewn out of lava, clay figurines and heads with the characteristic, curved Mayan nose.

The Doctor is an enthusiastic amateur, but he has little notion of the relative value of the pieces he showed me.

"Here," he beamed. "I found these myself near the pyramid of Chalchuapa." He pushed a half-dozen chipped and weathered heads toward me. I clucked over them dutifully and turned my attention to several of the really beautiful jars.

"Oh, those," he shrugged. "The Indians around the volcano open old tombs and pull out that sort of thing whenever they need a few *colones* for *guaro*. They bring them to me, knowing I'll give them fifty *centavos* each for the best ones. Take a look at the work in this piece."

He unfastened his gold watch chain and passed it to me. The fob was an exquisitely carved stone in bas relief depicting a man and woman kneeling face to face on either side of a gigantic corn stalk. Hieroglyphic bird, animal, fish and snake

43

motifs filled the background. The stone was beautiful, but it was mounted in a crude, baroque clasp of silver, obviously designed by the local jeweller.

A patient knocked at the front door just then, and the Doctor disappeared into his clinic.

"Your husband has some beautiful pieces," I ventured to Mrs. Rojas.

"Alfonso and his hobbies," she smiled and shook her head. "The garage shelves are filled with more jars gathering dust." She dismissed the subject and looked at me directly. "I understand you're a writer, Mr. Wolff."

I modestly allowed that I was. My past pursuing me again. Worse, she insisted on my recounting the themes of each of my novels, all so unutterably far behind me now. However, she being beautiful and I being human, I dwelt at some length on the success of my first book and skipped lightly over the gelatinous impact the other two had on the reading public.

"I wish I could read your books," she sighed. "I'm afraid I'm terribly envious of anyone who is creative. The world must look so new and fresh to your eyes."

I didn't want to tell her how the world has looked to my eyes during the past few years, so I shrugged noncommittally. She, of course, mistook it for modesty.

"Tell me about your new book," she begged. "Will it be about Central America?"

"Yes," I lied once again and raced on, improvising wildly. "It's a sort of parable about modern man, sick of soul and uncertain of his values amid the confusion of a tawdry, smoke-grimed society. He seeks a pause, a peaceful parenthesis, in the surroundings of a more restful, tradition-bound culture, in order to rediscover himself and chart a new course for the future."

It sounded to me as empty as, in fact, it was, but she murmured:

"How interesting, Mr. Wolff. Do go on."

Well, I couldn't go on, of course, because there wasn't any more. In fact, there wasn't even that. So I hedged, telling her that it was still in the formative stage and that I had a writer's superstition about talking out my ideas before setting them down on paper.

"Of course," she said, "I understand. But if you get a chapter or two finished before you move on from Santa Ana, I'd love to read anything you'll let me see."

"Naturally," I promised gallantly. "You'll be the very first to see it."

And I made my escape, wiping invisible beads of sweat from my forehead.

What was it Mother saw in Frank? Was she attracted by his worldliness, the aura of the successful author? Or did she feel, perhaps, an instinctive maternal impulse that went unfulfilled in her relationship with Dad? I'll have to start at the beginning.

Chapter Six

October 31, 1931

I opened my eyes this morning to see a circle of fragmented light dancing on the overhead. For a few seconds I was ten years old again, back home in Oregon, awakening to see the shadow of grape leaves etched in morning sun against the bedroom wall. But as I surfaced into wakefulness, I realized that something had happened since then. The intervening years pressed down; I became aware of the ship's roll; finally I remembered where I was. An unfamiliar sensation gnawed at the edges of consciousness. I lay quietly, waiting for the thought, watching the circle of wave-reflected sun from the port like a cat eyeing a mousehole.

It came to me at last: it was the very fact that I was alert, fully alive, on awakening. For the first time in years my head was clear, my tongue uncoated; anguish was absent. I waited for my nervous system to start clanging like a fire bell, but it didn't. I stretched in the bunk, relishing the peaceful feeling.

The odor of fresh, strong coffee curled into my stateroom, pulling me out of bed and under the shower. Dress is casual aboard the *Pamela D.* — shirt, dungarees and sandals. Within fifteen minutes I was shaved, clothed, and at the breakfast table, swarming over my orange juice, papaya, ham and eggs, toast and coffee, like a cloud of Egyptian locusts.

The unfamiliar tingle impelled me out on deck after breakfast, led me up to the bridge to check our position on the chart, prompted me to loiter and watch the deckhands remove the forward hatch cover, finally furnished the whim to strip down to swimming trunks and stretch out on a blanket here in the lee of the funnel with the self-satisfied air of a man who has put in a good day's work.

The sun drills into me, drawing perspiration through my skin. It is a clear, salty liquid that beads my forehead and gathers in rivulets that run down my chest to stain the blanket. A few months ago, I think, it would have been a gummy, yellow wax with the lingering odor of empty beer bottles and wet cigaret butts. It burns through me — the sun — vaporizing ego, volition, desire, and leaving only the drowsy pull of baking flesh and lax muscle. I lie here, de-energized, hypnotized by the slow rise and fall of the ship and by the iridescent flying fish which spurt from the blue walls and glide through the air to splash and disappear into the water again. This moment is as empty as air. I glide through an instant that hangs suspended outside of time, hoping only that it will be a long flight, that I will clear the next wave and the next, before one rises with a blue shock to pull me back into the carnivorous depths.

How far back do the bottles lead? All the clear, brown, black, green empties with gay labels I have drained and tossed aside? A chain of dead soldiers run back through the years, through thousands of blurred episodes, like clues in a manic paper chase. Drinking, at least in the beginning, was a gesture of defiance for an Oregon preacher's son: an act of liberation from tanktown mores, from the entire national ethos spelled out by Congressman Volstead. It opened the door on Prince Charming, who had none of the Puritan inhibitions which hobbled my everyday flesh: a debonair personality who took Dadaists, Surrealists, shaggy Bohemians and nature-fakers in tipsy stride and spoke on equal terms with the Big Name writers and painters whom the small-town boy secretly envied and sought to emulate.

Other people can take a drink or two and stop, but I can't do that any more. The thirsty worm in my brain whispers hoarsely, imperatively, for another and still another. Why should that be? Ah, Frank, didst know the reason, then hadst unriddled thyself and, discarnate, been subsumed into featureless Nirvana.

That may not come to pass for thirty or forty years yet, provided my liver holds up under the past decade's pickling. Meanwhile, I lie here wondering idly what to do with myself in the interim. The sea slides past me in hushed, oily swells, and I gaze out at the flat, blue horizon. Some essential part of me seems to have slipped through my grasp during the past, incoherent years. Perhaps it was no more than illusion, youthful optimism, but I feel dimished by its loss. It is enough now to close my eyes and offer myself up to the sun, to immolate my portion of being in fire and emptiness.

I know Frank's feeling. Despite Paul and the children, I too feel that rudderlessness, that sense that I have lost something vital, that the horizon is closing in.

November 2, 1931

Between fits of the shakes and midnight onslaughts of invisible insect armies, I lay in the sanitorium and thought about myself, my past, the wreck I had made of my life, and I wondered what sort of future I might be able to construct. During one period I found myself drifting farther and farther back in time, sliding at first in free revery and impelled later by a conscious attempt to learn exactly where I had taken the wrong turn. The search became an obsession, a means of escape from my white-walled prison and prickly thirst.

I circled and hovered over the desert of my past like a dispassionate buzzard marking my own staggering tracks in the sand past one remembered landmark after another. From that objective altitude, it was clear that my marriage and all that followed it was a wasteland; I was already a lost cause when I settled in Paris after the war. I winged back, searching for a touch of green in the landscape, hunting some hopeful oasis from which I might possibly have struck out in a different direction rather than plunging along the path that had led undeviatingly to my sanitorium bed.

I found the oasis finally in that postwar summer after my only year in college, when Virgil Harris, Johnny Hayes and I had hired a string of mules in Sonora, California, and packed into the Sierras along the north fork of the Tuolomne River.

We had elaborated a project of panning for gold up where the streams are born from glacial ledges, higher than anyone had ever tried before. Our explicit goal was to come back with enough gold dust and nuggets to pay the coming year's tuition; secretly, I am sure, each of us aimed at nothing more than a carefree summer in the mountains.

We loafed along with the mules, following the river upward, stopping now and then to fish for rainbow trout in some likely spot. In the late afternoon we would camp in pine-scented meadows where enraged chipmunks danced on high branches and chattered at our intrusion, where spotted deer came out at dusk to graze on the far side of the clearing. We pushed on and upward for a week, fording tributaries and following animal runs through the pines wherever the river whitened and ran bankfull through steep gorges. The air grew thin and sharp; poppies and daisies gave way to blue lupine and snowflowers; the river itself dwindled to a brawling creek that hid under boulders in the ravines or lost itself in meadowgrass.

Finally we burst in on a natural bowl where a glacier had died during some past ice age. Its terminal moraine had pushed up a natural dam, behind which a green lake mirrored three gray peaks with snow blanketing their shoulders. A flower-dotted meadow fringed the lake with lighter green, and an abandoned log cabin, built years before by some misanthropic aesthete, stood on a spur of rock jutting out into the lake.

We unpacked, hobbled the mules, swept the cabin and moved in, unmindful of the fact that mud had fallen away from the chinks and there were gaps in the roof where shingles had blown away.

All three of us were searching for something more than gold, I think. At night, after a dinner of venison, beans and coffee, we would sprawl atop our sleeping bags around the dying coals in the fireplace while brittle cold seeped into the cabin through the chinks and the disordered roof.

"A man's a fool to stay on the farm or waste his life away in a small town nowadays," Johnny told us. "This country's gonna grow like Iowa corn now the war's over, but no dirt farmer or country storekeeper's gonna get his hands on any of the big money. I'm heading for New York as soon as I can. That's where this country is run from. How 'bout you, Frank?"

What was it I answered?

"I'll try newspapering here on the Coast for a while," I think I said. "I'd like to work up to a foreign correspondent's job after a few years and see as much of the world as I can. Then I'd like to write about it."

Virgil remained silent, poking at the coals with a stick. We both waited for him to speak.

"I don't really know what I want," he finally said in his shy, hesitant way. "I'm not a big-money man like you, Johnny, and I don't feel much call to go skittering around the globe like Frank here." He paused and stared into the coals. "I'd like to do something useful, though, something I felt was important. I just don't know what it is yet."

We turned in, and I don't remember that we talked any more about our dreams and uncertainties. Neither did we find any gold near the lost lake, although we scrambled around at the foot of glaciers with our shovels and broad, shallow pans for the next two weeks. We finally broke camp when our provisions ran low and we had grown tired of eating fresh venison twice a day. We wound back down through the river gorge with butcher birds fluttering above us, mimicking the tinkle of the mule bells.

We stopped at noon the second day on a grassy flat where a small stream joined the growing river. Virgil methodically built a fire and started boiling water for coffee. I rigged a casting rod, and Johnny got out his gold pan and started washing sand along the tributary. I had landed a good-sized trout and two middling ones when Johnny, out of sight upstream, let out a whoop. We dropped everything and raced to where he stood peering into his pan. Despite his unsteady hands, we could make out two or three dull yellow grains in the black sediment that were clearly not the false, glittering pyrites.

We forgot about lunch, about the mules, about everything but gold, and we spent the rest of the day working along the stream until it was too dark to see what was in the bottom of our pans. That night we devoured my trout and some undercooked beans without knowing what we were eating. Sleep came late. Even after we had exhausted speculation about our potential wealth, we would drag each other back from the borderlands of consciousness with inane outbursts across the dying coals of the campfire.

Next day, Virgil found the first pothole in the early afternoon. For centuries a rounded boulder had ground its way into the stone creekbed, leaving a circular depression choked with sand. He struck his shovel into it by accident and washed out a dozen grains and several small nuggets in the first panful. We gathered around, dipping out the remaining sand and pebbles with tin cups and finally scraping the bottom with frozen fingers to retrieve the last nugget and grain of gold. After that, armed with pointed sticks we waded barefoot in the icy water, prodding the bottom until the stick sank into another hidden hole. By the third day we were convinced we had exhausted every pothole and riffle along the small stream, and we had two-and-a-half poke sacks full of dust and nuggets.

We had run out of beans and coffee and were growing gaunt on a diet of trout and wild blackberries, so, despite Johnny's protests, we packed the mules once again and headed for Sonora in three forced marches. On the way down, Johnny rambled on deliriously about coming back with placer equipment to search out the vein of gold. Maybe he did just that; I don't know. When we arrived in Sonora, we cashed in our treasure, divided it three ways, and I returned to Oregon briefly to pack, say goodbye to my parents, and buy a steerage passage for Paris.

That decision, from my vulture's eye viewpoint, was what led to my undoing. To thrust myself into the embrace of the age-old, experience-wearied whore of Europe at the age of 21, set in march the chain of events that led me to the sanitorium.

Frank went off adventuring; so did Papa Manuel and Dad. Mother, on the other hand, was exiled in Santa Ana all her life and died imagining Paris from what she had read and from the descriptions of others.

"It's strange, Carmen," she says as we walk along the street, "I've lived here all my life, but I've always felt as if I'm only passing through Santa Ana, as if I don't really belong here at all. Sometimes when I look at my sisters, at friends I've known all my life, they seem to be from another country and to speak a language I don't understand. When I go into my bedroom I'm surprised to not see my bags standing there, packed and ready to leave."

She frightened me when she said such things. At that age I equated departure with death — what other way was there to leave Santa Ana? — and I imagined her lying in the coffin (it's only been a week now) with two candles burning at her head and two at her feet.

"I know that someday I'll find the place, the city, where I belong," she continues, but I stop listening, because I can only see her lying dead in her black box.

November 3, 1931

I decided in the sanitorium that I had to return to the shores of that lost lake and start all over again, ignoring gold that might lie in the bottom of fast-running streams, in best-selling novels, in Hollywood. Fired by my new-found conviction, I drew up a long list of provisions and supplies ranging from wedges for splitting firewood to ten boxes of shotgun shells. I also wrote Johnny and Virgil during this flare of enthusiasm: two inane, "what are you doing now?" missives, they were, which carefully avoided explaining my own sanitorium address. I had a hunger to establish contact

52

with that lost paradise, I suppose, an anxiety to reassure myself that it really had happened once upon a time. I never did get a reply from Johnny.

I planned to arrive at the lake in September and spend a month cutting and splitting firewood, chinking the cabin, replacing the missing shingles. I would stack the wood high under the eves, lay in a store of pemmican and salt fish, and wait for the long nights and the snow that starts falling in early October at that altitude.

I wanted to winter there with deer, squirrels, rabbits, birds — and no bottles at all — for company, and only an occasional cougar track for news. I would start writing again when the lake froze and the snow drifted down through the jackpines. I would be far, far away from headlines, breadlines, smokeless factory chimneys, and the grimy, staring windows of the poor. The sun would come up each morning behind the three gray sisters to the east, silhouetting them, fringing their profiles in ragged gold, spotlighting the blue-green curtain of pines on the opposite slope behind the cabin. I even outlined in my mind a ponderous, unsaleable lyric of simple forest creatures — one of them myself — hibernating, nuzzling stored nuts, drowsing in warm, hollow trunks or well-chinked cabins while the blizzard raged outside.

Doc Adams characterized this as my Walden Pond phase and pointed out that a man who had geared his life to Paris and Hollywood would probably go out of his mind if snowbound in an isolated mountain cabin for an entire winter.

"You had better think it over carefully, Frank," he warned me. "Look behind the wish, and you'll find you are still trying to escape reality."

I did think it over after my original enthusiasm had thinned out a little, and I was forced to agree with him. But it left my basic problem unsolved: it happens that I just don't like "reality" as I've experienced it. Reality is a chaos of cities, buildings, streets, buzzing with swarms of unknowable people. I observed, when I was still very young, that the

53

world was peopled with incomprehensible, vaguely menacing beings, most of whom were much larger than myself. Learning to read helped somewhat, and the world of school and books diverted my attention from real people for a good many years.

When I became intrigued by writing, I dealt with people by taking them apart and reconstructing them in words, much as I had taken old alarm clocks apart and reassembled them when I was younger. This manipulation depersonalized them; it was a way of keeping them at arm's length and of avoiding direct, emotional contact with them. I dealt with words, not with humans, and whenever I was threatened by unseemly, raw emotions, I learned to escape into the bottle.

Even my marriage to Carole wasn't a genuine emotional experience. She was a symbol to me: the glittering debutante daughter of one of the old-money families along Philadelphia's Main Line, and very fashionable in spite of, and because of, that. To all appearances, she had rebelled against stodginess and liberated herself to study painting in Paris. I suppose she saw me in much the same light: the phenomenally successful young writer — also a fashionable rebel — who seemed destined to write one blazing novel after another for the rest of his life.

But marriage brings people too close together for superficial illusions to long endure. Carole prodded me, peered at me through her sharply-focussed Philadelphian lorgnette, and discovered that I was only an uncertain Oregon boy with an accidental success behind me and years of torturing self-doubt ahead. For my part, I soon discovered that her Montparnasse apartment was not nearly as ascetic nor as Bohemian as it appeared at first glance, that her paints and canvasses were, in reality, stage props which slowly sprouted a patina of dust while we circled at a dead run from newly-discovered *avant garde* bistros on the Left Bank to tastefully redecorated 18th century drawing rooms on the Ile de St. Louis.

All this I pondered in my hospital bed. It was amusing to watch Doc Adams gird himself for his daily battle with my recalcitrant archangel. He was a dogged, head-down counterpuncher, but he was no match for me. I had parried and danced away from the anxious thrusts, the tentative jabs and good advice, delivered by dozens of better men than he. Had I not wearied of the farce, I might be there yet, stretched out on his leather couch, mentally circling out of reach of his forebearing silence and alert pencil.

Chapter Seven

Frank's candor, his brief enthusiasm to find his way back to his mountain paradise, gives him the wistful air of a lost child; irony adds the precocious cynicism of a child who had set aside his innocence reluctantly.

Mother taught me to think that the only thing which stood between me and certain triumph was the deadening atmosphere of Santa Ana itself. My optimism started leaking away drop by drop only after I arrived in Washington as a student. Mother herself faced life in Santa Ana with pliant resignation after her illusions slipped away, but Dad, on the other hand, always retained his innocence, continued to dream of returning to Nicaragua, of seeing Central American unity achieved, with all the enthusiasm that Frank invested in his lost Sierra lake.

"When I finished high school in León," he tells us, "I came to San Salvador to study medicine. I found a room in a *mesón* and went out to look for work the next day. The first thing everyone asked me was:

"Where are you from?"

"'Nicaragua,' I would tell them.

"'There's no work here for you *Nicas*.'

"And from that day to this I've fought for Central American unity."

For years Dad has spent his free hours writing speeches and articles, sending bales of telegrams to the five presidents urging them to take this or that step which would further the cause of unity. In his office there are boxes full of news clippings, letters, communiqués, grandiose projects for overthrowing the Somoza clan.

"I'll live to see those bandits out of power," he has repeated for years, and ever since I can remember he's

56

contributed money to one abortive revolutionary plot after another.

"Don't be foolish, *viejo*," Mother would plead with him. "You're throwing away money we need. Don't you see those people are opportunists? They exploit you with their great plans, and then they laugh behind your back."

But Dad kept on giving money without telling Mother, kept on watching one scheme after another fall apart, kept on making empty plans to return to his boyhood home.

Unlike Dad, Mother lost her innocence somewhere along the years. At times she had traces of adolescent mischievousness; spontaneous laughter would bubble from her throat after a small prank. But usually her expression was grave — her Indian look, Dad called it — and her gestures were measured. She seemed, when she thought nobody was watching her, to be searching deeply within herself.

I remember the trip to Yucatan. It was my first airplane ride: San Salvador, Guatemala, Mérida. Mother and Eugenia took me with them. I trembled and held my breath as the earth dropped away below us, giggled as we split through the cotton clouds. The earth became a rumpled, green blanket criss-crossed with the brown stitching of roads.

I was fourteen years old, and the thing between Mother and Frank had ended long before; she brought her memories along on that pilgrimage. (Why did she leave the diary for me to read? Why didn't she burn it and leave me with an unmixed image of her?) Suffocating in the heat, we caught a bus from Mérida to Uxmal and rode across the flat, baking landscape, wedged in amongst baskets of live chickens, bundles tied with henequen twine, white-clad Indians who stared blankly out the windows. Dust boiled up behind us in a semi-solid cloud.

At Uxmal I climbed to the top of the Dwarf's castle, gazed out over the monotonous, shrub-dotted plain, and gingerly picked my way down the crumbling steps. I had my picture taken sitting on an impassive reclining idol; the stone basin resting on his stomach had once held palpitating human hearts. I walked through the patio of the Nuns' Palace, fingered the intricate mosaic of its walls and stroked the elephantine nose of Chac, the rain god. The heat was unbearable at noon, even in the shade. I remember we killed three scorpions in the small, thatched hut where we slept.

I was awe-struck by that dead city, but I couldn't understand the alien forms: a series of mudpies, perhaps, created by the children of some weird, nonhuman deities in the course of their afternoon play. It was not until months later that Don Chico convinced me that the Mayan civilization had really been erected by a race of living, breathing human beings like myself and that their blood ran in my veins.

I remember Mother poised, straight as a lance, at the edge of a *cenote*. She bore herself with the air of a Mayan princess about to be sacrificed, hurled with a weight of heavy gold bracelets and precious jewels into the watery arms of Chac waiting below. I was hurt because she had been ignoring my puerile chatter, and I thought spitefully that she cut a ridiculous figure standing there, high above the water, with her head back and her eyes closed. Now, of course, I know she was listening to Frank, here in the patio, telling her:

"There are enormous cisterns, great natural wells called *cenotes*, half-filled with milky green water. The Mayans sacrificed their most beautiful virgins in those pools to assure a good crop during the coming season."

Chapter Eight

November 4, 1931

The sea is filled with immense jellyfish. They bob along just below the surface, and the ship slices through them like a plow cutting a furrow through a field of translucent mushrooms. We've been at sea long enough that I'm beginning to feel kinship to the Ancient Mariner. It may be that, like him, I peered over the side today and blessed the jellyfish, unaware. At any rate, I haven't felt the albatross about my neck, it's dry feathers tickling my throat, all day long. I'm beginning to take this feeling of well-being for granted, along with the other mundane miracles of sunlight, fresh air, and the sea. I don't entirely trust this reaction — it may be part of a plot I'm hatching to catch myself off guard — but I shall accept it conditionally for the moment and pass on to other matters.

I've hoarded enough strength by now to start taking stock of my present situation. The time has come, for example, to face the fact that I'm sitting in mid-ocean aboard this decrepit, rusted freighter, bound for nowhere in particular, merely because of a whim. That it was whim born of emptiness and despair cannot justify it nor lend it any special significance.

Let me return to the morning I walked out of the sanitorium. Spiritually, I felt like a convict whose term has been shortened for good behaviour. I had been thinking about the future, but only in long-range terms, not in niggling detail as to what I would do from minute to minute after my release.

Doc Adams had a few parting words for me: the moral equivalent of the ex-con's shabby suit and ten dollar bill.

"You know enough about yourself now, Frank," he told me, "to never smell a cork again. Just follow that rule, and you'll get along fine."

59

I was freer than most men ever are when I walked out of there, no doubt about it. I had no family at all, no job nor any pressing need to take one. Most of all, though, I had no desires, no ambitions, no clearly marked destiny to fulfill. I was an extra pawn in the cosmic chess set. As I stood on the curb waiting for a taxi, I felt as rudderless as a cloud borne on the passing breeze, and as evanescent. It was an unbearably empty sensation; man is a spiritual battery yearning for a positive, or even a negative, emotional charge. Like nature, he abhors a vacuum.

A taxi pulled to the curb. I tossed my suitcase in and climbed after it. I had a momentary impulse to drop in on Barry Logan, who had stored the belongings from my apartment at his place. But what did I have there? A few suits and a few dozen books, perhaps. My long fling with John Barleycorn had reduced my material impediments to practically nothing. Besides, no sooner had the impulse flashed across my mind than it was followed by a disjointed montage of my last evenings with Barry — the parts of them, anyway, that stood out above the fog of drunken amnesia. A few examples: I lie on my back on someone's living room carpet, babbling happily and gesturing with an empty Coca-Cola bottle that seems to be irremediably stuck on one forefinger; Barry patiently maneuvers me, boneless and giggling, into his car for the drive home; and just before the blackout on that particular night, I lie on my bed, fully clothed, kicking playfully at Barry as he tried to get my shoes off. No. Barry had earned his freedom.

"Take me downtown," I told the driver. As we rolled along I realized that I hadn't a single friend to turn to anywhere. I had worn out all my welcomes months and years before. Even the buzzing sycophants and freeloaders of Hollywood had abandoned me when it became clear I was on the skids. There was no one I could call on the telephone without getting an embarrassed pause and a flimsy excuse. A hard-working dipsomaniac like myself doesn't have any real friends; he cuts them out of his life, spitefully in an infantile tantrum, or in

60

shame and relief so he can return undisturbed to the only thing that really matters: that next drink.

In this mood, I became aware that for the past half-dozen years I had not given enough of myself to any person that I could now lay an emotional claim on someone in return. Nobody anywhere cared enough about Frank Wolff even to sit down patiently for an hour or two and listen to his hard-luck story. By the time my cab ride came to an end, Doc Adams' psychic folding money had been spent, and my spiritual raiment had shrunk to the dimensions of a loin cloth.

I registered at the Biltmore. I didn't pick up the telephone, didn't even consider going back to Beverley Hills or Hollywood. The studio had informed me through a lawyer that they had cancelled my contract for nonfeasance and had deposited a good-sized cash settlement in my bank account. I had no intention of contesting that decision; I didn't want to face any of them again. I sat at my window most of the time, watching the knots of unemployed congeal, swirl, drift apart, and re-form across the street in Pershing Square. I went out for meals from time to time. I bought newspapers and sat on park benches to read them. I bought popcorn and peanuts to feed the pigeons, also from park benches, and I went to the movies every day. Then I returned to my room, stretched out on the bed, and fought down the desire to have just one drink to cheer life up a little.

This went on for nearly a week. I could only read so many newspapers and magazines a day, or see so many movies, before the gray tedium began to drift in like Los Angeles smog. I couldn't write at all — didn't even try — and I could think of no place in the United States that might alter my dark dreariness. I was a burned-out light bulb, but my nerves whipped me raw inside, night and day, as I lay immobile in the bed.

At some point during this period I got out Virgil's letter and re-read it. My letter to him had been forwarded, probably by his parents, and a few days before I left the sanitorium I received an answer from him postmarked Santa Ana, El

61

Salvador. He informed me he had become a lay preacher in some evangelical sect and was now working as a missionary. My God! I thought, he's turned into a religious fanatic! With that, I had dismissed him and his letter from my mind.

Now, however, mired in the intolerable, grimy emptiness of Los Angeles, I began remembering my year in Mexico, my fascination wih the old Mayan ruins in Yucatan, my half-formed resolution at that time to learn more about that exotic, dead civilization. It was the first flicker of anything resembling interest or motivation I had felt since my release, and I spent most of several days in the public library reading about the Mayans, southern Mexico and Central America.

Virgil's letter didn't say much about the country he was living in, but there were a few snatches of leafy green and volcanic cones in his prose that reminded me somehow of our summer together in the Sierras ten years before. And perhaps, as an apostate son of a preacher, I had a morbid urge to find out what kind of person he had become, to try to decipher his reason for dedicating his life to God. His letter was matter-of-fact, not stuffy or sanctimonious; perhaps it would be possible to talk to him.

I decided on the spur of the moment to go to Central America, tour the Mayan ruins there, and then swing back through Mexico to see how the Revolution had fared since I last looked in. I would surprise Virgil, dropping in unannounced to spend a few days enroute to Honduras and Guatemala. I found passage on the *Pamela D.*, a freighter leaving San Pedro for Panama a few days later. To date, the trip has turned out to be better therapy than anything Doc Adams provided.

November 7, 1931

The seafaring portion of my Odyssey came to an end this morning when I carried my single suitcase ashore at La Libertad and caught the little, toy train to San Salvador. I arrived here with no previous prejudices, nor any firm plans as to how long I might stay, but I was immediately depressed. The lush green vegetation visible from the train window, the volcanic cones on the horizon, promised an exotic tropical paradise, but San Salvador shatters the illusion...

The jet dips a wing toward Lake Ilopango, and the horizon straightens out again slowly. Panchimalco's single file of huts along the road, the white smear of San Salvador's buildings against the green, humped back of the volcano. The plane touches, slows, and turns ponderously toward its parking area. Alfredo there on the terrace, but alone, wearing dark glasses. She's dead! Too late, too late. She's dead. Last time at least thirty of the family, Dad and Mother in the center, waving and laughing as I came down the steps. Dead. Never, never to see her again.

"Salvadoreans first. This way, please, ma'am."

He watches me with curiosity, watches tears trickle down under my dark glasses. The heat is good — dulls me like a tranquilizer. And the keys? I can't find them. The keys she always carried...

"That's all right, Ma'am." Nothing fits in my purse. And the exit? Which way?

"Your baggage pass, lady."

"I can't find it."

"All right, go on through."

"When did she die?"

"Last night. She wanted to see you, but.... The funeral's at five today."

"I tried my best."

"We didn't expect it. She breathed twice and was still."

"I'll never see her again."

"Fine. Everybody's just fine."

"Be careful! The truck!"

San Andres is in flower, just like last time.

"It's always so beautiful here," she told me." Look at the blossoms on the *maquilishuat*."

63

"Colón already?"

"We've made good time; it's not twelve yet."

A bus blocks the road ahead.

"*Pupusas de lorocos,* Miss. You want some? With cheese and sausage."

"No, buy mine. Here you are."

They crowd around the car, sweaty-faced, baskets filled with *pupusas*, fruit, buzzing flies.

"Look at these," one thrusts a crusted hand through the open window. "*Jocotes de corona.* Or you want some mangoes?"

"No, Carmen," she always said, "you can't have any. Everything's so filthy."

The bus starts off, and we pull away from the milling, shouting women.

Chapter Nine

"Niña Carmen," María interrupts, "Niña Celia and Niña Meches are waiting for you in the patio."

There they are, the two of them, planted like monuments: poker-stiff, bulging with fat, dressed in black.

"How are you?" they greet me in chorus and struggle out of their chairs simultaneously. They seem glad to see me; it's getting harder every day to make conversation with Dad.

"Thank you, Meches, for the lovely flowers you sent to the *novena*. They still look fresh after a week."

"My! You're looking more and more like your mother!" Celia exclaims." Why, my heart skipped a beat just now when I saw you walking down the corridor." Dad looks through me with vacant eyes and says nothing. His rocking chair creaks, creaks, creaks.

"I'm so glad you like them," Meches continues." I went up to Santa Clara to pick them myself. Weren't the gladiolas lovely? They won a prize last year in the fair at San Salvador. They're from the United States, you know," she turns to Celia." Julia brought me the bulbs, and every single one of them sprouted. It's the climate at Santa Clara."

"How long will you be staying?" Celia asks me.

"I'm not sure. Probably another month."

"That's wonderful! The Doctor won't be so lonely that way."

"Why don't you go back with Carmen for a few months when she leaves?" Meches addresses Dad. "It would do you good to get away."

"No," Dad answers wearily, "if I leave Santa Ana, it will be for Nicaragua. If not, I'll just wait here."

"Sarita is finishing high school at Asunción this year," Celia announces, "and I'm thinking of sending her to the

States. Do you know of a good nuns' school in Washington, Carmen?"

"No, but I'd be glad to find out for you."

"You'd be doing me a great favor. And perhaps Sarita could come and visit you once in a while if it's not too much trouble."

"Why, of course, Celia. We'd be glad to have her."

A nuns' school! And she'll spend her weekends visiting people from the old home town. Why do they bother? She could learn English here just as well. She'll come back with the same prejudices reinforced, and she'll inject English slang into her conversation to show she's been away. Meches has forgotten her German by now, and that's all she had to show for five years in Munich. Now it's the United States that's fashionable. If I lived here, I'd never send the children up there for their education.

"I'm glad you married Paul," Dad tells me. "He's a good husband: a hard worker, no vices at all."

I suppose Dad is right in a sense; Paul is a good husband if, by that, you mean a good provider. He fills the house with kitchen machinery, air conditioning, television. He'll give me anything I want that works by pressing a button. He never argues about the abstract reproductions, the contemporary furniture I choose, though I know he would prefer heavy, overstuffed chairs he could sink down into, massive mahogany tables, paintings of landscapes or flying birds. He should have married someone else.

Neither of us realized how difficult it is to build a bridge between two cultures, two backgrounds as different as ours. The religious difference was never a real problem; neither of us held any intransigent attitudes about that. What drove the wedge between us more than anything else was our different nationalities. At first, whenever we discussed the Latin American policy of the United States, each of us was sure that the other would eventually come around to his viewpoint.

66

Now, years too late, I can see that all the arguments only led each of us to harden his own position. I suppose I had a prejudice, as Paul claims, but he agrees more than ever with anything Washington does to Latin America. If he ever doubted that his wonderful democratic institutions were infallible, his whole world would come down around his ears. And of course his newspapers never lie, and all the big monopolies are only in business for philanthropic reasons.

"Ah, if I could only quit and concentrate on my painting," he sighs and runs his fingers through his crew cut. He's been saying the same thing for years, and at first I believed him. "But," he gives a martyred shrug, "we have to think about the children's education, you know." It's a pose he assumes for my benefit. Paul wouldn't dream of becoming an artist even if he were guaranteed twice his present salary. An artist in the States is an odd, suspect character, and Paul wants more than anything to feel that he is a solid, respectable citizen.

It's strange; Mother never talked to me much about Paul, never asked questions or offered an opinion. I wonder if she noticed? I always did my best to make it appear...and Paul liked her and was good to her. Besides, they hardly spoke to each other. She was shy about her accent in English, and he never has learned to speak Spanish. He claims he doesn't have the time.

Mother liked Washington: strolling through Rock Creek Park, visiting the National Gallery and Philip's, window-shopping in Georgetown. I guess I felt the same way at first.

"You're so lucky!" she would exclaim. "All the opportunities you have here." And I would feel a pang. She was sure we would turn out differently just because we had gotten away from home. Just like Celia. It didn't work, Mother. You should have let me stay here, let me shift the blame to Santa Ana.

It might have been different in Paris. Everything in the States seems so synthetic. Or maybe if Paul had been more like Frank...I don't know.

"You're too emotional, Carmen."

67

But my hair goes straight up when I hear him and his friends speak of "God's country." God's country! With Negroes treated like animals! God's country, with its smug sense of superiority to the rest of the world! God's country, with its mania for material gadgets and its signs that warn: "Gentiles only."

"I think there's a Sacred Heart school in Washington," Celia addresses me. "Haven't you heard of it?"

"No, but I'll find out as soon as I get back and send you the brochure."

"Before you leave," Meches interrupts, "you'll have to come and see the house I gave Lito and Tere. I have my own room there whenever I want to spend the night. You'll see how beautiful it is, and the garden too. Of course, it cost a fortune! We brought roses from England and some weird plants that Lito wanted from India. There's a swimming pool..." her plate slips and she pauses, twisting her features to gum it back into place, "...for the children, since we're lucky enough to have water. It's the only place with a well on the whole mountainside. Imagine what luck that was, Doctor!"

She turns to me again.

"You'll just have to come, Carmen. You'll love it. We brought the stone facing clear from Guatemala, and all the bathroom tile, the rugs, furniture, everything, came from the United States."

"My goodness, yes!" Celia chimes in. "It's a real palace. Lito doesn't realize how lucky he is to have such an aunt."

"The only bad thing," Meches continues inexorably, "is that the back patio where we have the pump is always filled with people coming to buy water. They're all so filthy! You should see what the wall looks like near the pump. Why, the other day there was even a woman picnicking with her kids under the *amate*. Lito had to send the foreman to throw them out."

"Ah, you can't do anything with those people," Celia sighs. "They're used to living like animals, and they dirty everything they touch."

"Sometimes I feel like taking out the pump," Meches says, "but it's a good business. Like I said, it's the only place with water in the whole region."

Dad looks through her and goes on rocking.

"I stopped by to see your great-aunts yesterday," Celia breaks in as María finally appears with coffee and pastries.

"Ooh! *Quesadillas!*" she interrupts herself with a delighted squeal. "And from Niña Conchita's bakery. Nobody can make them the way she does."

I pour coffee, and Celia takes up the thread of her conversation.

"Poor Ginny is as blind as a bat now, but she's still as marvelous as ever. She was punishing St. Anthony again when I was there — had him turned around facing the wall for some reason..."

The little house was different when Mamita María was alive: always filled with children, music, flowers. She played the piano and would have us sing for her. She kept a trunkful of pictures, costumes, and unexpected trinkets for us to play with. For our birthdays, she would give Alfredo a kaleidoscope or a piñata she had made herself; she would give me miniscule books she manufactured, filled with aphorisms painstakingly cut out, word by word, from the newspaper and pasted into the tiny pages.

Even when she was bedridden a few weeks before her death, she would joke wih me when I came to visit her after my tennis lesson.

"Do you want to read me another chapter?" she would ask avidly, pointing to the book on her night stand. It was *Gone with the Wind*, I remember, and her eyes would sparkle at Scarlett O'Hara's mischievousness.

69

"It's terrible of me to let a thirteen-year-old girl read a book like this," she would worry out loud, but then she would wrinkle her nose and chuckle:

"You just can't imagine, Carmen, how much that Rhett Butler resembles your Papa Jorge."

"How is Cata?" Meches breaks the ritual silence of coffee and *quesadillas*... "I can imagine how she must have felt when your mother died. She's been with you about thirty years, hasn't she? Ah, she's a jewel!"

"No, you don't find treasures like that Cata any more," Celia sets her cup down. "The kind of help you find these days is just terrible. Why, I pay my cook sixty *colones* a month, give her an afternoon off every week, and still she complains! Believe me, I'm going to get rid of her one of these days. A creature like that is never satisfied with anything you do for her."

If they don't leave soon, I'll explode. How could Mother stand it? Everything is the same as it always was. Worse. Everything is sliding away, wearing out; nothing ever happens. Days, months, years, don't mean a thing; there still isn't a single bookstore, theatre, or restaurant. Nothing to do but drink, if you're a man, or gossip and complain about servants, if you're a woman. One little blind world on top of other narrow, choked worlds below: the seven, self-destroying circles of Santa Ana forming a motionless inferno.

Mamita María's daughters, Virginia and Lola, huddle like dank mushrooms in the small, dark house, waiting for death. Wilted, shrunken, they drag themselves through the rooms, surrounded by cats, smelling of cat, making their weak tea and dunking bread crusts in it, incapable of sparing a thought for anyone else, hoarding their remaining days of meanness and squalor like misers. It was Mamita María whose presence lighted that house; Mother who lighted this one.

70

Now that she's gone, Dad has collapsed — even Dad, whom I could never imagine losing his vitality, his determination to bend life to his terms. The plants will go to seed; weeds will spring up in the patio; the closed rooms will become mildewed; dusty cobwebs will sprout in the dark corners.

Alfredo hasn't the strength to hold things together. Last time when I came with Paul and the children to spend Christmas here, Alfredo had already gone dead inside. He walked into the house on Christmas Eve and stared at me with bloodshot eyes.

"Where's Ana?" he asked. "Thought she was already here. C'mon, le's go get her."

We roared through the narrow streets, hurtled across blind intersections.

"Be careful, Alfredo, please."

"Ah, nobody dies 'til his time comes," he grins vapidly through the windshield. "Anyway, it'd be better if I did. Black sheep of the family. Your good-for-nothing brother. The old man's always sore at me; hardly speaks to me any more."

We swerve at unchecked speed to miss a pedestrian.

"Know what? Early this morning I knew I was gonna get tight. Sure enough! Ran across a drinking buddy across from the Cathedral, and we've been sitting in the Florida ever since then. How 'bout that?"

He laughs with loose lips, and we swerve and stop screechingly in front of his house. Ana is watching us from the balcony. She calls to him, but he pays no attention. He pushes the door open and disappears down the hall. Ana comes down the stairs, and we kiss the air formally over each other's shoulder.

"Where are the children?"

"I made them take a long nap after tea, because they'll be up late," she answers distractedly, "but Chon should be getting them dressed now. Let's go and see..."

A pistol cracks deafeningly from the bedroom. We race down the corridor, sharing a single thought, and stumble over each other opening the door. Alfredo, sitting on the edge of the bed with a pistol in his hand, laughs mockingly at us.

"Whassa matter? Scare you?"

"What's the matter with you, Alfredo?" Ana hisses as anger washes out the terror in her face. "Have you gone out of your mind?"

"Big cockroach over there," Alfredo aims unperturbedly at the wall. "Got 'im right in the head."

Two of the children, wild-eyed, crowd into the room.

"Go sit in the car," Ana orders them with trembling voice. She gropes for the door blindly as tears fill her eyes. "Don't you have any shame? What kind of Christmas are you giving your children?"

The door slams behind her, and Alfredo looks at me. Behind the loose-lipped mask, in the depths of his eyes, lurks a terrified appeal.

"Don't you start in now." He puts the pistol back in the drawer of the night stand. "You'll see. One of these days I'll aim in the right direction."

The rocking chair creaks, creaks, creaks, in counterpoint to Meches' shrilling.

"Did you hear that Lydia González' daughter got married in Mexico?" she calls. "They say the boy is a real catch: from a good family, rich, has a profession. A good Catholic too. Ah, it's so true, the old saying: 'Beauty would fain have the luck of the plain.' That scrawny little Lydia's a fright. And her sister, Gloria, is such a pretty girl, but can she find a husband?"

Maybe I'm going dead too, dying a little more each day with Paul. There's less and less to say to each other with each year that passes. And his superior attitude, ending each quarrel with:

"You're too emotional. It's impossible to discuss anything with you."

I know. I am emotional. That's what life is, isn't it? It isn't just logic and triangles and parallelograms. He sees me as some kind of a doll, pretends to know all my reactions in advance. If he'd only treat me like a human being, we might be able to save something of our marriage.

Oh, I've tried all the *Ladies' Home Journal* things: I greet him with a cheery smile when he comes home, take his coat, bring him his slippers, pretend to be interested in whether the stock market is up or down. But he never notices. He's always the same: he answers in monosyllables, slumps into his easy chair and hides behind the newspaper. What is there left to save?

"Hello! Hello!" Dr. Selva's bulging stomach precedes him through the doorway, and he nods formally to each of us. His eyebrows are white now, but his hair is a piebald thatch of brown, black, silver. Dad comes alive for the first time as the Doctor proffers a ceremonious handshake upon Celia, Meches, and myself. He claps Dad on the shoulder.

"I've come to challenge you to a game of billiards," he announces. "We've missed you at the Casino; the boys have been asking about you."

Dad smiles.

"Sit down for a while," he says. "We'll see about it."

"How is your family, Carmen? Have you heard from Paul?" He doesn't wait for my answer, but addresses the others:

"Have you heard that Colonel Gutiérrez just died?"

"Really?" Celia cries. "The poor man! He was sick such a long time. But he's going to have a magnificent funeral."

"Oh my yes!" Meches shrills. "I've heard that General Sisniega himself is coming from San Salvador."

"Remember, Dad," I interrupt, "when you stopped the Colonel from beating that prisoner in the street?"

73

He nods slowly.

"May he rest in peace," he replies, "but the Colonel was a very hard man."

"Had the uprising already taken place when that happened?"

"Yes," Dad straightens in his chair, "it was right about that time, and the National Guard was making arrests by the thousands. There were many abuses."

"Everyone in Izalco trembled whenever the Colonel would appear," Dr. Selva recalls.

"Of course," says Meches. "I'd forgotten you had a clinic in Izalco at that time."

"Yes," he affirms, "right where it all started. I was serving as coroner there besides running my regular practice here. Colonel Gutiérrez will have a good deal to answer for when he faces St. Peter."

"May God forgive him," Celia answers stoutly. "You have to remember what he did for the country. If he hadn't organized the Civic Guard, we might all have had our heads chopped off."

"Excuse me, Celia," Dad looks squarely at her, "but there were a lot of common murderers in your famous Civic Guard. Terrible crimes were committed on the pretext of defending the country."

"How can you say that, Alfonso? The Civic Guard was made up of boys from the best families. Your own uncles," she juts her chin at me, "were in it, Carmen. Hmph!"

"You don't remember the things that happened, do you, Carmen?" Dr. Selva asks me.

"How could she?" Dad answers. "She was barely seven years old."

"It was terrible!" Dr. Selva shakes his head slowly. "And it was much worse in Izalco than here, of course."

"Did you know Martí?" I ask.

"He was the criminal!" Meches shrieks. "He was responsible for the whole thing."

74

Dr. Selva purses his lips, but Dad leans forward impatiently.

"I must contradict you, Meches," he says firmly. "I was a friend of Farabundo's, and he was no criminal. He was Sandino's secretary and a brave man. He may have been mistaken, but he lived and died for what he believed in."

"Remember, Alfonso," Dr. Selva interjects, "they shot those two boys, Luna and Zapata, along with Martí. Poor Luna was only twenty and recently married when he was executed."

"They got what they had coming!" Celia glares at him. "Crazy youngsters, pretending to be saints before they understand anything about life. Peasants and shoemakers and beggars are where they are because they're no good for anything else. The Colonel and the others did what they had to do to save the country."

"There's only a handful now in Izalco," the beggar woman tells Mother and me, "only a handful of us left." She looks down at her bare feet.

"Come along, Celia. It's time we were leaving." Meches rises and shakes herself like a ruffled hen. I accompany them to the door with a false smile. They embrace me huffily and hammer off heavily on their heels. How could Mother stand them?

"Terrible, terrible things," Dad recalls, rocking back and forth slowly. "Some of the National Guard units couldn't be trusted, and Colonel Gutiérrez put Perico Ramos in charge of a truckful of troops headed for Izalco. Perico told me about it afterward: he was obsessed by it.

"'Suddenly,' he said, 'we were stopped by a log across the road and a band of peasants with *machetes* behind it. I told the machine-gunner to open fire, but he wouldn't do it. I pulled out my pistol and killed him, and then I handled the machine-gun myself. I had two of the others lift the log away, but there was no time to clear away the bodies, and we had to run right over them.'

"Perico never got over that," Dad taps his forehead. "He was never right up here until the day he died."

"Were you in Izalco that day?" I ask Dr. Selva.

"Not until the next day," he replies. "I was here in Santa Ana. Remember, Alfonso, it was raining ashes here all during that time?"

"Colonel Gutiérrez called me and told me there was a problem in Izalco and that they needed my assistance. That was all he said. He gave me a truck and four guards to get there.

"When I arrived there was a young lieutenant waiting for me. He was pale.

"'Where are we going to bury all these people, Doctor?' he asked me. 'We're afraid the water supply will be contaminated.'

"He took me to the main square where they were piling the dead like cordwood. I looked at the heaps of bodies, with arms and legs sticking out here and there.

"'In the wasteland at the foot of the volcano,' I told him, and that was all I could say."

"That was how Martínez put himself in power for thirteen years," Dad sighs "And he seemed like such a quiet little Indian."

"He was a Theosophist, Carmen," Dr. Selva turns to me. "He wouldn't kill a mosquito or a cockroach, but people were a different matter." He shrugs and gets up from his chair.

"Let's get along to the Casino, Alfonso. We have time for a game or two before dinner."

Chapter Ten

It's the first time I've been alone in the house since I arrived. Six o'clock: the gossip hour. A haze of scandal hovers over Santa Ana's patios:

"Haven't you heard? Josefa's daughter was at least three months along when she got married. She was simply "bulging under her wedding gown..." The waspish buzz rises over the rooftops.

Mother herself never took an active part in relaying gossip, but she listened to it — you have no choice in Santa Ana — and it stuck in her mind. When Paul and I brought the children to spend Christmas here, I was curious to learn what had become of friends and schoolmates I hadn't seen since leaving for the States, and I asked her about them. She had occasionally mentioned one or another of them in her letters to me, but now, in answer to my questions, she ticked off a rosary of family tragedies, scandals, infidelities, and public or private failings which had marked the lives of almost every one of my childhood friends. I had forgotten how efficiently the Santa Ana grapevine functions, and I was shocked. Her words painted an enormous Hieronymus Bosch canvas containing hundreds of detailed figures frozen in the midst of monstrous, perverted acts.

"Good heavens, Mother!" I finally said, "you make Santa Ana sound like Sodom and Gomorrah."

She nodded.

"It's terrible to learn these things about people you've known all your life: to understand at last that everyone is imperfect, that each of us would fall if exposed to the exact temptation he was unable to resist."

"There's no privacy here," I protested, "it's worse than the monkey cage in a zoo."

"'Small town, immense inferno,'" she quoted with a gesture of resignation. "I know you think I'm overly pious

77

these days, Carmen, but I find that the Church is a real comfort. Perhaps it's not the right answer for you; you're still young, and you have many other interests. But I find that I need it."

She paused reflectively for a moment.

"Perhaps I wouldn't feel that way if we had moved to San Salvador. I always wanted to, you know, but your father would never listen to me. There are people there — Don Lino, Augusto, Alberto — one can talk to: people with the same interests. Here there's no one." She smiled apologetically. "Your father is a wonderful person, Carmen, but we don't find much to talk about now that you and Alfredo have grown up and moved away."

The voices drone on:

"Poor Josefa! Troubles never come singly. Her Miguel doesn't care what people think. He takes that half-breed mistress of his shopping in San Salvador, and they go parading right down the main street. I hear he's even bought a house for her."

There's a moment's silence and a sigh. The sighs are part of the ritual.

"And what's happened to Neto Orellana? The last I heard, the police were hunting for him in Sonsonate..."

They go on as they did yesterday, as they will tomorrow in the patios of Santa Ana. The sunset is red. It's burning time in the hills.

Chapter Eleven

...It is an ugly, squatting city of frame houses roofed with corrugated iron sheets. The few substantial buildings of brick masonry are webbed with cracks, fraught with the threat of impending collapse. The entire city has the improvised air of a refugee camp thrown together by the survivors of some great catastrophe — which, in fact, it is, as I learned from the owner of the hotel where I am staying. The eruption of San Salvador's volcano fifteen years ago was accompanied by a series of earthquakes which left the city a shambles. Since then, the survivors have used only the lightest building materials, and no edifice is higher than one story. My own hotel is nothing more than a creaky, wooden shed built around a central patio, with French doors leading into the separate cubicles.

I ate a heavy, grease-saturated lunch a few hours ago and strolled through the town afterwards with uncovered head. It was an error. The only trees to be found are in the small park before the cathedral (which also has a corrugated iron roof). The sun beats down relentlessly in the narrow, dusty streets. There was almost no movement during the siesta hour, and I found nothing to prick my curiosity or even hold my attention. I returned to the hotel with a rock-crushing headache and a growing conviction that the whole trip has been a terrible mistake.

A cold bath drove away the headache, and now I lie inert on the metal cot imagining a fat-fingered bartender wiping the collar off a schooner of beer and sliding it down the counter into my waiting hand. I can feel the wet coolness refreshing my fingers. Thousands of miniscule bubbles, each one bearing its iota of malt perfume, stream upward to bury themselves in the base of the foam glacier. The image is more real than the room in which I am lying, with its high, discolored ceiling, its unshaded lightbulb suspended from a wire that runs across the ceiling and down the wall to the switch beside the flimsy door.

The beer is as real as my thirst. What is unreal is the light filtering through the green shutters of my unscreened window, the tepid air oozing through it like thin glue, bearing me olorific hints of garbage, fly-dotted feces, and a pungent, sweet stab of something that may be rotting fruit, frangipani, or a whore's perfume, for all I know.

That I should be lying here is neither more nor less absurd than that I should be anywhere else. That my tongue and throat should be prickling with dust and the desire for a quart of ice-cold, foam-covered beer, is customary and in no way remarkable. What is incredible is that I can be coldly conscious of the torment, holding it at arm's length in my mind, so to speak, without submitting to its thrumming bass imperative, and that I can go on at the same time fabricating a clarinet solo of contrapuntal words and phrases in this notebook, like a Tibetan guru immolating himself in flaming yak butter while his pineal eye remains unwaveringly fixed on the cosmic panorama of constellations and galaxies pin-wheeling along the ecliptic.

November 10, 1931

Virgil insists that I move in with him during the remaining few days of my stay in Santa Ana. I'm stranded here until Saturday when a bus leaves for Guatemala, but I'm not enthused by the invitation; since escaping my father's awe-inspiring presence I have scrupulously avoided all association with the God-annointed. On the other hand, I've spent the past months in solitary confinement munching on my own liver. It may prove a useful discipline in my erratic program of self-rehabilitation to force myself to spend a few days with somebody whose views arouse in me an instinctive antipathy. In any event, the Hotel Florida here is even more distressing than the hotel in San Salvador.

Speaking of rehabilitation, I've made no progress on the problem of what to do with myself. My mind is set, cramped in fact, with the determination that I will not start drinking again. All right. But that's a negative resolution, not a program of action. I've reread the pages of this notebook and have found in them nothing more than listless, narcissistic introspection: certainly no hint that the great American novel is germinating in some unused recess of my brain. I suppose I will continue to set words down on paper as a form of occupational therapy, but writing — writing a book that will be read by pimple-squeezing adosescents, dyspeptic high school teachers, by bored ladies in penthouses who nibble chocolates or stroke a Pekingese while they read — that is a different matter.

I'm a man with no occupation, a victim of mental and emotional bankruptcy. There's no point lingering outside the gate, coat collar turned up, hands in my pockets, gazing dumbly at the "No Help Wanted" sign. I must find something to do, or at least let something vital happen to me. Then I'll have to learn all over again whether or not I have anything worthwhile to say about it and whether or not I can find the exact, effortless, inevitable way of saying it.

November 13, 1931

Virgil was seated at the table with his Bible and his bilingual dictionary, mumbling and snorting and making heavy weather of rendering next morning's sermon into Spanish, while I was stretched out on the extra cot, thinking as usual about my own tenuous foothold in an unpredictable universe.

Virgil writes his sermons out in English first and then laboriously translates them word for word into Spanish — a language he approaches cautiously, as one would approach, let's say, a domesticated panther. He would look up occasionally and consult me about a turn of phrase, each time jarring my wispy thought pattern to shreds. However, I recognized in his interruptions the professional courtesy of one writer to another, and I answered him patiently, generally encouraging him to preserve the construction he had already hit upon. To my mind, the syntactical anarchy and erratic tenses of his translation added enormously to the metaphysical lustre of his message, and I looked forward to watching him in action, to gauging the effect on the congregation of his passionate glissandos and table-thumping denunciations of sin, all in broken Spanish.

There came a knock on the door. Virgil answered and, after a brief exchange with a barefoot peasant, turned to me with Christian resignation.

"Let's go and look at some hogs," he suggested.

He slipped the unfinished sermon into his dog-eared Bible and rummaged under the cot for his veterinary's satchel. I got up and said *Buenos días* to the caller, who bobbed his head at me, grinned, and scratched the top of one caked foot with the horny big toe of the other. Virgil pulled the door closed behind us, and we followed our visitor through the burning, mid-afternoon streets of the town, lagging farther and farther behind to allow the rich odor of pig dung which enveloped him to attenuate before we walked through it.

A group of children playing in the entrance to a *mesón* stared at us with shining, almond eyes and excited grins. They were uniformly dirty, uncombed and snot-nosed; and the youngest were stark naked. When we were safely past, they shouted at us in unison:

"*Gringo! Gringo! Vaya al Chipalcingo!*" Screaming with laughter, they darted into the security of their communal compound.

Virgil gestured helplessly.

"Did you notice their swollen bellies?" he asked. "A parasitologist would have enough work to keep him busy for three months just with those six kids. I sometimes think I must be crazy, wandering around nursing hogs or cattle and horses while these people are dying like flies all around me. I'd bet my shirt that half the babies born in this country die before

82

they're a year old. And those kids back there — the ones who have survived — are riddled with hookworm, tapeworm, roundworms, chiggers, malaria, and dozens of things we've never even heard of in the States. I know they never see milk or meat. It's a wonder any of them grow up."

He strode along, head down, oblivious to the scorching sun.

"You don't know where to start," he continued. "I talked to Don Herminio, the mayor, about it once.

"'Can't you at least give sandals to the school kids so they won't get hookworm?' I asked him. He laughed and told me it would take the entire national budget just to buy shoes for everybody who needed them in this country.

"'Besides,' he said, 'you give them sandals and their daddies would sell them next day to buy *aguardiente*. You can't do anything for them,' he told me. 'You'll learn you're wasting your time.'

"I don't know what to do." He made the helpless gesture again. "I feel like a criminal when I treat pigs with medicines these people could never afford to buy for their own children. I try to talk to them. That's all I can do, and maybe it helps a little. After all, in the beginning was the Word."

I automatically stop listening as soon as the first religious cliché comes rolling out, so I looked around at the outskirts of Santa Ana, seeing them for the first time. The unbroken, block-long adobe walls of the houses had given way to barren lots where goats grazed and scrawny, long-legged chickens pecked. The jungle rolled in from the countryside, overwhelming the individual thatched huts with their prickly stockades of cactus.

Our guide was as far ahead as before, but the pig perfume was growing more authoritative, and I deduced that we were approaching the piggery. The road widened suddenly, and we came upon a crowded Saturday marketplace where shawled women squatted patiently behind mounds of oranges and other unfamiliar fruits heaped casually on gunny sacks. Two or three carts displayed bright printed cloth, cheap combs and mirrors, packets of needles and thread. There was one cart with pails of yellowish and pink liquids and a row of dirty glasses arranged uninvitingly on a counter beneath a smudged banner which proclaimed:

"Refresh yourself — 5 *centavos*." The hub of this commercial activity was a general store, a dark, little *cantina*, and an open-air butcher stall with flies blackening the strips of meat hung above the counter. The proprietor of the stall came to meet us, wiping his hands on a blood-caked apron. Most of the people in the marketplace were eyeing us curiously.

"Good day, good day," the butcher shook our hands heartily. "They're back this way."

He led us off the road and through a fringe of banana trees behind the butcher stall. Some of the idlers in the square followed us and took positions around the pigpen. The butcher fumbled with the knotted rope which held the gate closed.

"There they are," he nodded. "Those three. They've been sick for two days now. Won't eat a thing."

A wrinkled old lady dressed in black suddenly materialized from among the banana trees, flapping her shawl like bat wings. She had no teeth, and I could scarcely make out what she was shouting."

"Don't let him in!" She hopped up and down in a frenzy. "He'll kill every one of them! The devil sent him! He's going to kill them all!" She made horns with the fingers of her right hand and pointed them at Virgil and me, trembling all the time with rage and fear.

"Stop it, Mama," the butcher said. "This man is an animal doctor. He's going to cure them."

"No! No! No!" she screamed, hopping up and down again and staying a safe five yards away from us. "The devil sent him to destroy the Church. He buys souls for the devil!"

The butcher sighed and pushed the creaking gate open for Virgil. The two of them walked through the slippery muck to the three animals lying on their sides. Other scrawny pigs milled and squealed in the far corner. The old woman leaned against the top rail shouting at Virgil and her son. Other sightseers, attracted by the noise, drifted in from the marketplace and gazed back and forth from the ancient Fury to the two men in the pigpen, like spectators at a tennis match.

Virgil squatted over a pig, thumbed its eye open, clucked his tongue, laid his hand on its neck, and carefully inspected its abdomen, while the butcher watched him anxiously. He repeated the performance with the other two animals, then stood up and looked around the pigpen thoughtfully.

"Aren't you going to give them any medicine?" the butcher asked. Virgil shook his head.

"It's a very bad disease," he explained carefully in pidgin-Spanish. "It is called hog cholera."

"Surely you can cure them," the butcher insisted. "I'll pay you for the medicine." Virgil shook his head again.

"You'll have to kill these three and burn them," he said. "We can try inoculating the others, but it may be too late."

The man sputtered.

"Kill them?" He waved his arms wildly. "Burn them? You're crazy!"

"See what I told you?" the old hag screamed. "He's going to kill all of them! The devil sent him! Make him go away!"

I don't think Virgil had understood a single word she said. His intake capacity in Spanish is limited to one person and a very few words at a time.

"You'll have to move the other pigs out of here as we inoculate them," he strained mightily to make himself understood. "Then you'll have to clean all this out," he gestured at the pigpen, "and burn the ground with gasoline."

"What are you talking about?" the butcher shouted over the prostrate pigs.

"He's trying to starve good Christians to death!" the old woman shrieked, making horns with her fingers again and squinting at Virgil.

"Have any of them gotten sick before this?" Virgil asked. The butcher looked down at the three pigs sullenly.

"That meat out there," Virgil gestured toward the butcher stall, "did it come from sick pigs?"

"Get out of here!" the man burst out. "I don't need your medicines."

"Go away!" the old lady seconded him. "Go back to the devil!" She stooped down suddenly and then hurled a piece of pig dung at Virgil. It struck him in the back, and the crowd laughed.

"You'll have to burn all that meat, too," Virgil said stubbornly, "You can't sell people infected meat."

"Go to the devil! Go to the devil!" the old woman chanted. She picked up a rock and threw it, missing him this time. There were dozens of people ringing the pigpen now, all of them laughing.

"Did you hear him?" the butcher appealed to the crowd. "This *gringo* is trying to ruin me!"

"Virgil!" I called to him in English. "This is getting out of hand; we'd better leave."

Just then a man near the gate laughed drunkenly, picked up an egg-sized rock, and caught Virgil in the shoulder blade. Virgil looked around dazedly, rubbing the spot.

"I'll have to report this to the health authorities," he told the butcher.

"You go to hell!" the butcher shouted, pushing him roughly toward the gate. The drunk picked up another rock, and I grabbed his arms.

"Hurry up, Virgil, for God's sake!" I called. I tried to reason with the drunk.

"Why do you want to throw rocks?" I asked him as he flailed about, trying to break my hold. Virgil, stumbling toward the gate, held up one hand.

"Please! Please!" he called in broken Spanish. "We are all sons of the same God."

"A son-of-a-bitch is what you are!" the old lady screamed. There was a milling crowd around us. The drunk wrenched away from me and swung around, snarling. Somebody kicked the back of my knees, and I went down. The

86

drunk snicked open a switchblade knife and hurled himself on top of me. We rolled over on the ground in straining, pummeling confusion. Then we were pulled apart, the drunk cursing and frothing, his knife lying on the ground. The small boys in the circle laughed and gestured excitedly. Whoever held me, turned me and pushed me headlong out of the circle. Virgil helped me up and we walked rapidly, almost running, through the banana trees and back to the main road. I staggered along in a daze, barely conscious of Virgil, who repeated over and over again:

"Where do you start? Where do you start?"

I became aware of a stitch in my side.

"Let's slow down a little," I pleaded. "I think we're away from them."

I pressed my hand under my jacket to ease the pain. It felt wet, and I withdrew it, staring uncomprehendingly at the blood that dripped from my fingers.

"I've got to sit down," I told Virgil, and that's the last I remember.

Chapter Twelve

November 21, 1931

I decided to accept Dr. Rojas' standing offer of a late afternoon chess match today. Mrs. Rojas greeted me with a firm handshake and a welcoming smile when I was ushered to the patio. I explained my mission and apologized for intruding.

"Not at all, Mr. Wolff," she replied. "Alfonso has been called away for a delivery, but he may be back at any time. Why don't you wait a while, and we can talk?"

"There's nothing I'd like better," I told her. "I've been leading a hermit's existence for too long a time."

"I can't believe that," she smiled, "but, of course you must find Santa Ana terribly boring."

I eased myself into a chair gingerly.

"It has had its unexpected surprises," I assured her.

She gestured at the house and patio with a resigned sweep of her hand.

"Here you have my world. It is just as narrow and circumscribed as these walls, and just as provincial and dull as Santa Ana itself."

I looked at the patio, gold and green in the afternoon sun, with warm blazes of flowers here and there; my gaze took in the white symmetry of the arches framing the garden, the cool, dark tiles of the corridor.

"I envy you all this," I said. "You're living in the Garden of Eden without recognizing it. It's the image of peace and tranquility I have searched for since I was expelled from my own Garden."

"When did that happen?"

"I must have been ten or eleven. It was a condition — a state of mind — rather than a particular place."

She laughed and shook her head.

"The grass is always greener on the other side of the fence. You would have to live in this so-called Eden a while before you noticed the weeds. You would have to let time work its way with you, watch the sun march across the sky and disappear each day, listen to women talking interminably about dresses and babies and parties, and to the men's sterile conversations about politics and next year's coffee prices. Then, little by little, you feel the roots pushing down through your soles, feel your arms turning into stems, your hands into leaves, your head into a flower that nods and wilts in the conversation."

"A very animated flower, Mrs. Rojas. No signs of wilting."

She accepted the compliment with a brief smile and went on:

"Life must hold more meaning than this small, dull round of activities that repeats and repeats and repeats itself day after day. A man like yourself is free to search for new experiences that give zest to living, but a woman..." She raised a shoulder hopelessly.

"If it's any help to you," I said, "an Indo-Chinese friend once explained to me that all this is merely illusion which each of us sets in motion by his desires. 'There is really no time nor space nor motion,' he told me, 'only an unmoving eternal present.'"

"Terrible," she shuddered. "That sounds even worse than Santa Ana." Our laughter established a subtle bond of complicity between us.

She frowned thoughtfully.

"That seems so hopeless. Do you believe the world is really as meaningless as that?"

"I might answer with an old Buddhist expression: *Quién Sabe?* And I might add, why worry about it? I draw humility from the thought that Buddha was sitting under his Bo tree pondering the Eight-Fold Path 2,500 years ago and that Indian Scholastics were chopping Buddhist logic while our ancestors were wearing blue paint and slaughtering each other with spears. Today we use machine-guns and poison gas, and we call it progress. Predictably enough, when our local Redeemer came along, we crucified him and fed his followers to the lions as a spectator sport."

"You're a pessimist, Mr. Wolff."

"I'm a pessimist, Mrs. Rojas. And please call me Frank."

"All right...Frank." She hesitated a moment. "And you may call me Isabel."

"We could benefit from the Eastern doctrine of nonviolence," I swept on, carried away by her brown eyes, her smooth, olive skin and her lively interest, "but whether we can adopt Buddhism or something like it in the Western world, is another matter. Having been born and raised in this particular pattern of illusion, I must adopt the prudent principle that it can eat me if I'm careless."

She laughed again: a delightfully spontaneous, bubbling sound.

"In other words, Frank," she summarized, "you sit behind your loaded machine-gun in the Lotus position."

"Exactly," I grinned.

The maid appeared at that point with a pitcher and two glasses on a tray.

"I don't know the details of the Eastern tea ceremony," she turned mock-serious, "but the Salvadorean tamarind ritual consists of handing a full glass to the guest. Or would you rather have a whisky and soda?"

"Oh, no! No thank you," I replied, much too forcefully.

She arched a jet-black eyebrow at me quizzically, and suddenly I found myself stammering out the whole story of my "problem," Hollywood debacle, sanitorium and all. Unbelievable *gaucherie* on my part, particularly after such a high-flown, intellectual beginning, but I couldn't stop myself. She sat listening to me, taking an occasional sip of her tamarind drink, and I arrived at the Los Angeles hotel interlude and was feeding the pigeons in the park before I could cut myself off.

"I'm sorry, Isabel," I apologized. "I don't know why on earth I should be telling you all this."

90

She wasn't laughing at me, though; her expression was serious, almost sad.

"So," she said finally, "Virgil is the only person you have in all this world, and you came looking for him."

"Why, no, of course not," I contradicted her. Then I paused to think about what she had said.

"Well," I corrected myself lamely, "perhaps you're right in a way. Virgil may represent a part of my past that I would like to recover."

"But he hasn't been able to provide any answers, and neither could your doctor in Los Angeles. Is that why you're trying to convince yourself that the world is an illusion and that you yourself are only a thirsty ghost?"

I grinned at her across the rim of my soft drink.

"You would make a great psychoanalyst, Isabel."

"That's too tangled a jungle for my taste," she shook her head firmly, "and I don't like the feel of your empty Oriental universe. No Frank, I'll have to hold on to my uncomplicated Catholic faith; that's difficult enough for me to live with."

That was that. I had regained my self-possession, and we began to talk of other things.

What did Mother feel at that time? How deep were her religious beliefs? Did she use religion as a curtain to shut out the emptiness and perversity of Santa Ana? As a compensation for the increasing loneliness of her marriage? There was a period — but long after Frank disappeared from her life — when she pored over Rosicrucian texts, practiced Yoga breathing exercises, and visited mediums to have her fortune told. She always took her own dreams very seriously. I remember her telling us one morning at breakfast:

"I had the strangest dream: so vivid I can still see every detail. I was walking along the street hand in hand with a barefoot gypsy girl who was dressed in a long, green skirt. She led me into a jewelry store and began rummaging through the display cases, pulling out one necklace after another to show

91

me. The sales lady was annoyed, and I was embarrassed, but the gypsy girl paid no attention.

"'Don't you love this one?' she asked me. 'Isn't it beautiful? Here, try it on.' I told her no, I already had enough necklaces. She laughed and led me into the street again. There she took both my hands and said:

"'You and I are the same person, but you are afraid of me because I need to live intensely. Don't be so afraid of things,' she begged. 'Don't keep me locked up all the time.'

"Wasn't that an odd thing for me to dream?" she appealed to Dad. But he only laughed and asked her to pass the sugar.

November 23, 1931

Eduardo picked Virgil and myself up early this morning in his Model T Ford, and we went gasping and rattling off to Izalco. I was curious to get a closeup view of the volcano which has provided a monotonous, kettledrum accompaniment to my life here during the past two weeks. The cone itself lies behind the shoulder of the dormant Santa Ana volcano and is not visible from the town, but a subliminal shudder, followed by the distant rumble of its eruption, jostles Santa Ana every fifteen or twenty minutes, day and night. According to Eduardo, it has been particularly active recently.

Virgil provided the principal motive for our trip. A young man named Farabundo Martí, whom Eduardo worships as a sort of Messiah, wanted some advice on modern poultry-raising methods, and Eduardo had suggested that he consult Virgil. Eduardo described Martí as one of those enthusiastic idealists who crops up now and again with a determination to reform the world. He has turned his coffee plantation into a peasant cooperative and apparently spends all his free time engaged in social uplift work in the rural areas. I was mildly curious to see how the two missionaries would get along with each other.

We had a gravelled road most of the way, so the trip was pleasantly dust-free. The highway bore a surprising amount of traffic: oxcarts laden with sacks of coffee berries, barefoot women stepping along gracefully with water jugs or bundles balanced on their heads, tiny donkeys almost invisible under mountainous loads of kindling wood or fresh-cut grass, and now and then a herd of lean cattle which choked the road and reduced our progress to a crawl. The panorama had an air of vitality and bustle, and I said so to Eduardo. He clucked his tongue dubiously.

"You see it with foreign eyes as a quaint, picturesque scene, Frank," he told me. "Try looking at it my way for a minute. Those cattle we just passed don't belong to the men who were herding them. Neither the coffee in those oxcarts nor even the carts and oxen themselves belong to the cart drivers. We are passing through Don Jaime Dominguez's estate just now, and almost everything you've seen along this road belongs to him. And everything in sight except the gravel, the telephone poles, and this car, remains just as it was 200 years ago."

He was right, of course. His words neatly singled out the common denominator of changelessness: one of the things I find most appealing about El Salvador.

I ventured that unemployment couldn't be as terrifying in a tropical country like this, where most people lived on the soil and raised their own food.

"I'd much rather be out of a job here than in the Chicago slums, where you have to buy groceries and coal and heavy clothing to survive," I told him.

My comment was a mistake. Eduardo bounced up and down on his seat and became nearly incoherent.

"Put yourself in their place, Frank," he sputtered. "Your country may have an unpleasant climate, but is it any more pleasant to die of disease or to waste away of vitamin deficiency than to die of cold? Could you stand to be treated like a burro all your life and watch your children grow up to be denied schooling and treated the same way? These people are human beings like you. Think of that!"

His fury startled me, but I had to admit he had a valid point. Since coming here, I've accepted the disparities around me as so many exotic elements of a pleasing picture painted for my benefit. I've been gratified at the sight of a ragged, barefoot man squeaking past in an oxcart, at the grace with which the women balance water jugs on their heads. But not until Eduardo's outburst had I paused to ask why women had to carry water that way, how far did they have to carry it, what quality of human existence could be achieved on the basis of oxcarts, water jugs and dirt-floored huts?

I apologized and attempted to placate him with a stumbling explanation of my new insight. Another mistake. Eduardo launched into another oration in which he prophesied the imminent and total collapse of capitalism throughout the world and warned me sternly, shaking a finger under my nose, that I would one day read in the newspapers about the liquidation of the fatted oligarchs of El Salvador and the triumphant establishment of a workers' and peasants' soviet. I soon lost the thread of his argument and limited myself to nodding in amiable agreement whenever he paused for breath.

The road straightened, and Izalco came in sight far across the valley we had just entered. As I watched, a fist of oily, brown smoke squirted up from the cone in slow motion. It rose, curling and writhing in upon itself, separated from the cone and hung in the air, a titanic mushroom. The wind carried it, slowly attenuating, out over the valley, and in a few minutes it was merely another ravelled cloud in need of laundering.

We arrived at the village of Izalco a quarter of an hour later. It's a neat, whitewashed little place, located at a discreet distance from the foot of the volcano. We stopped at a fountain beside the main street to refill the radiator, and I got a close look at the volcano: a perfectly symmetrical, ash-gray cone with no trace of vegetation on its poisoned flanks. It looms above the one-story tiled roofs, a constant, brooding presence, visible from every point in the town. Many of the Indians, according to Eduardo, are convinced it is the home of Chac, the

94

Mayan rain god, who sits inside rumbling and thundering to himself at the iniquitous ways of the white men who have stolen his people's lands.

Izalco erupted just before we set off again. From our new vantage point, only a few miles away, it was a shocking display of elemental violence. Eduardo felt the tremor first as we stood beside the car, and he tapped me on the shoulder. The ground shuddered underfoot and I wheeled to see a dark jet of smoke and ash shooting skyward from the crater. At close range the upward velocity of the cloud was dizzying. Huge masses of lava the size of cottages cartwheeled out of the column, crashed outside the rim, and rolled down the steep slope leaving smoke tracers to mark their passage. Then the noise of the explosion overwhelmed us in a sustained Niagara roar.

"Chac is angry at you," Eduardo grinned, shouting to make himself heard. "He doesn't like strange palefaces intruding in his domain."

We set off again, passing under the smoke cloud on the outskirts of town, and we arrived at Martí's plantation in another fifteen minutes. Virgil's meeting with Martí was undramatic in the extreme. The latter embraced Eduardo, shook hands with me amiably, and without further ado led Virgil away to the site of the future chicken farm. Eduardo and I tagged along, listening for a while to the discussion of chicken runs and chicken coop architecture, and I was glad enough to submit to a tour of the experimental farm under Eduardo's enthusiastic guidance. I trudged along beside him through fields where wornout coffee trees were being uprooted to make way for corn and beans, looked into the patient, brown eyes of the cooperative's milk factory and offered her a sympathetic "Moo!", and eventually we found ourselves back at the ranch house.

My mind was fixed agonizingly on the unattainable bottle of cold beer, and I was grateful for the substitute that Martí provided us: *cocos* with their tops lopped off by three deft strokes of a *machete*. The liquid inside was cool and had a refreshingly tart aftertaste.

"What do you think of my five-year plan, Mr. Wolff?" Martí asked me with a smile.

"It's a very interesting experiment," I replied. "I wish you luck."

His expression turned serious.

"We need it," he answered. "Luck and time, but most of all we need time. Our peasant masses are coming to realize that they can assert themselves through organization, that they can at last demand a change in the social structure. Last May Day, for example, we had a crowd of 90,000 who came in from the countryside to parade through the streets of San Salvador." His gaze was direct, penetrating. "Think of it! That's more than the entire population of the capital, and they were demanding the right to organize."

"The coffee planters and the military aren't standing still, Farabundo," Eduardo interrupted him. "There have been secret conversations in Santa Ana; I'm sure they are planning a coup."

"I know! I know!" Martí gestured impatiently. "There is bound to be a reaction from the oligarchy. There'll be repression and violence. Our people are passionate and impatient." He shook his head thoughtfully. "Time is the problem. Time and organization."

Virgil was seated at a table sketching a plan for chicken coops. I seized on a lull in the conversation to go and sit on the steps of the porch to sip my coco water slowly and look at Izalco rumbling and puffing above the coffee trees.

We returned to Santa Ana with Virgil wedged into the back seat amid cocos and stalks of bananas that Martí had pressed upon us.

"What do you think of him?" Eduardo asked me in a tone that allowed only one reply.

"I hardly talked to him, but he seems intelligent and very sure of himself," I temporized. "How about you, Virgil? You were with him longer than I was."

"Well," Virgil answered reflectively," we didn't talk any politics, but he sure is interested in taking care of those chickens."

On the road back I learned that Eduardo had studied for a year in Paris while I was living there. We swapped reminiscences of the Boul Mich and St. Germain, tried vainly to establish whether or not we might have rubbed shoulders in some Left Bank bar or cafe. We dropped that finally, and I persuaded him to talk about his family instead of politics for a change. I learned that he and Isabel were three steps apart in a family of eight children, who ran the entire gamut, as he put it, "from schoolteachers, bank clerks, and devout Catholics, to atheistic, hard-drinking revolutionaries like myself."

Chapter Thirteen

December 3, 1931

This afternoon when I crossed the park for the ritual chess game at Dr. Rojas', I noticed a group of soldiers lounging about the fountain in the center of the green square. There were two sentries on duty outside the National Guard barracks across the street from the Doctor's house, and several trucks were lined up inside the barracks gate, their drivers slouched against the fenders.

"It finally happened," Alfonso greeted me. "The army overthrew President Araujo this morning."

I commented on the unusual number of troops on evidence, and he nodded.

"Soldiers from Zapote fortress in San Salvador surrounded the presidential palace at dawn and arrested Araujo in his nightshirt. So far, nobody seems to have opposed the coup, and Colonel Gutiérrez across the street has been behaving as though he had just won the lottery."

Don Manuel, who usually doesn't arrive until after 6 p.m., was sitting in his special chair in the patio. He shook his head philosophically.

"Every country gets the government it deserves in the long run," he said resignedly. "Obviously, El Salvador deserves to be governed by a semiliterate Theosophist rather than an elected president."

I raised a questioning eyebrow, and he explained:

"It's clear that the coup was organized by the vice president, General Martínez, who also happens to be the ranking general in the army. You'll see: he will be declared president within the next few days."

"Pah!" he exhaled explosively. "The man's an ignorant Indian, and his wife's an ex-laundress."

Alfonso threw back his head and laughed.

"He really is an idiot," he agreed. "His son died of a ruptured appendix about six months ago, because the General refused to permit an operation. He was treating the boy himself with some kind of blue waters." He shook his head wonderingly. "Can you imagine such a thing: treating peritonitis with magic in the twentieth century? Our next Minister of Health will probably be a witch doctor."

December 6, 1931

I accompanied Virgil to his Sunday service this morning. It was held in a warehouse behind Don Vicente's leather tannery on the outskirts of Santa Ana. There were perhaps thirty people waiting for us. Some sat on benches and boxes placed haphazardly about the barren shed; the rest sat or squatted on the concrete floor. They all stood up when Virgil led off with the Lord's Prayer and then sat down again before he launched into his oration.

"In the beginning was the Word," he began (and here I attempt a literal translation from his Spanish). "The Word was in God, and the Word was God. God had invented Adam and had extracted Eve from the rib of the former. But he soon recognized with great sadness that they were imperfect and that, the minute he turned his back, they had eaten of the Forbidden Fruit, which was the Apple of Consciousness.

"With the first bite of that Apple the two of them lost their innocence. Eve blushed when she saw she was naked, and she went off to dress herself in leaves. Adam dressed himself also. When God saw them walking around clothed he told them that without innocence they could no longer remain in the Garden of Eden.

"The lily is unconscious of its loveliness," Virgil gave a sudden, disconcerting twist to his discourse, "and the bull and the lion do not know that they are fearsome and terribly beautiful. . ."

An old man seated beside me nodded emphatically at this statement.

99

"...They just exist, and the bull feels no guilt when he gores someone, nor does the lion feel badly when he has killed and eaten another animal. This is because they are Unconscious, and they cannot find the pathway to God because Conscience cannot find its way into them. They do not have access to the gift of the Word, which is the last present the good Lord granted Adam and Eve before expelling them from the Garden.

"We, who are all children of Adam and Eve, carry within us the Consciousness of our imperfection, which is a living wound." He struck the table emphatically. "We carry with us the Word that punishes us and prohibits us from being Unconscious, Innocent, like the animals. . ."

Well, I think that's enough. Virgil rambled on passionately and wrathfully for another half hour, turning page after page of his handwritten text while babies cried until they were nursed and the children nudged each other and giggled. I noticed that he made a chopping gesture with one hand whenever he came to a capitalized word, and he peered at the congregation from beneath his eyebrow at the end of each sentence. I'm certain — almost certain — that nobody understood what he was talking about.

When he finished, everyone stood up and started singing a hymn in Spanish. It was, to my great stupor, "The Little Brown Church in the Vale," with lyrics translated and adapted by Virgil himself. After that was over, everyone stood still until Virgil had posted himself by the door. Then they filed out, and Virgil shook hands with each of the grownups and patted each of the children on the head, just as my Dad used to do after the Sunday morning service in Willamette.

Very sardonic, Frank. But what about your own dream of a lost Garden of Eden in the Sierras? The wistfulness of the last sentence betrays you again.

100

If I could turn time back, I think I'd choose to accompany Dad and Alfredo again on one of our all-day hikes up the side of the Santa Ana volcano. We would drive as far as the road could take us and set off on foot beyond the highest reach of the coffee plantations. Huge, mossy trees shaded us from the sun, and in the open patches knee-high grass laden with morning dew would wet my legs and the hem of my skirt. Sometimes cotton-wool clouds covered the upper part of the cone until midday as we climbed, single-file, through gray mist with the trees and shrubs on either side standing out in silhouette like Japanese etchings.

We would picnic beside the sulphur lake inside the crater, and the sun would strike through the clouds, turning the water emerald green. When I tired on the way down, Dad would carry me piggy back and recite the rolling, florid verses of Rubén Dario as he trudged along. It would be nightfall by the time we returned home, dirty and scratched. Alfredo would hammer impatiently at the bathroom door as I dozed langorously in a warm bath, and afterwards the three of us would demolish the huge *arroz con pollo* Mother always prepared for those occasions.

December 10,1931

Some entries back in this journal, I admonished myself to be on the lookout for new and vital experiences. This country seems to offer vital experiences aplenty, but a high percentage of them are nearly lethal. In short, I am flat on my back again, this time with an acute intestinal infection.

The latest chapter in the serial misadventures of Frank Wolff, ex-drunk and sometime writer, began last Tuesday when Alfonso called for me, as he had promised, to show me another, closer view of the Izalco volcano. He had to visit a patient at Lake Coatepeque, and he suggested that we drive on around the lake afterwards and up to Cerro Verde, a high bulge on the slope of Santa Ana volcano. He guaranteed that from this spot we could look down into the crater itself from less than two kilometers away. It sounded as though it might be an unforgettable experience — and it certainly was, in an unanticipated way.

I had felt quite queasy the day before and had swallowed some horse pills that Virgil confidently prescribed. Alfonso came by so early the following morning that I had no time to take stock of my physical state until after we were on our way. We took the same road that Eduardo, Virgil and I had followed to reach Martí's plantation, but when we turned off the smooth gravel onto a rutted, dirt road I became aware that something was seriously wrong. I tried to convince myself it was due to the fact that I'd eaten no breakfast.

We rattled along through the coffee groves, my discomfort increasing with every passing moment. Eventually we jolted around a curve, and Lake Coatepeque spread out below us — an immense volcanic crater half-filled with blue water. Alfonso stopped with a jerk.

"What do you think of that?" he asked. I looked at the scene dimly, recognizing that to the objective eye it must be a charming view. My every bone ached; my skin was as sensitive as though I'd been flayed; my stomach churned and surged.

"Beautiful," I muttered. "Will you wait for me a minute?" I went behind a coffee tree out of his range of vision and vomited up my heart and lungs. I returned to the car with a shaky expectation that things would improve now. Alfonso looked at me curiously, but made no comment. He released the hand brake and we rolled down along the inside rim of the crater toward the lake. As we careened downward in neutral with the motor off, Alfonso waved a casual hand past my nose.

"There's a spot out there by the island where a hot spring comes up from the bottom of the lake. With a little patience, you can boil eggs in the water there."

"Very interesting," I managed.

We reached the edge of the lake and followed it past occasional resort homes and a ramshackle hotel that boasted a dock and a few tethered rowboats. The realization that I was not feeling any better grew into an overwhelming conviction. Alfonso turned in at the gate of a coffee plantation which stretched up the slope away from the lake. He stopped in front of the house with a jerk that left me gasping and took his medical bag from the back seat.

"Would you like to come in with me?" he asked.

"No thanks," I turned on a feeble grin. "I'll sit out here and look at the lake."

As soon as he disappeared into the house, I stole the center section of his morning paper and headed for the coffee grove. Once among the trees I stumbled into a half-trot, beads of sweat standing out on my forehead. A friendly farm dog galloped in rings about me, wagging his tail.

"Go 'way, dog," I muttered between clenched teeth. "Go 'way and leave me alone." I doubled over and vomited, then straightened up and stumbled on through the rows of trees until I found a secluded place. My legs trembled violently, and my clothing chafed my skin intolerably. When I finished I was as empty inside as a bell jar, but my intestines still coiled and squirmed like a canful of angleworms, and my stomach persisted in trying to force its way past my throat. I leaned my forehead against a shade tree and retched miserably until the world stopped rocking. After a while I shambled back to the car, telling myself that things certainly had to get better after *that...*

I slumped down in the seat and closed my eyes. The interior of the car had rearranged itself into sharp edges and uncomfortable angles that prodded my elbows, knees, the back of my neck. I wanted desperately to lie down in the back seat, but it seemed like an unmanly thing to do and, in any event, a move would require too much physical exertion. I wiped the cold sweat off my forehead, squirmed into another position, and closed my eyes again.

After an aching, nauseated aeon I heard Alfonso bidding cheery goodbyes at the door of the house, and I struggled to an upright position. He opened the car door and peered at me.

"You look a little pale, Frank. Are you sure you're feeling well?" he asked as he climbed behind the wheel. I grunted.

"The road to Cerro Verde is usually all right this time of year," he informed me as we bucketed along, "but later on in the rainy season you can only get through in an oxcart or on horseback." I noticed apathetically that we had left the lakeshore and were climbing the inner rim of the huge crater again.

"After we get to the top, we'll have to leave the car and hike a kilometer or two to get the best view of Izalco," he announced as if he were making me a gift. The world through the windshield was a crazy blur of trees and shrubs, dust clouds and oxcarts that streamed backward past us. The car jolted and jerked mercilessly. Alfonso is one of those drivers who lunges at obstacles and overrides them with grim determination and a heavy foot on the gas pedal.

From deep in my mind I dredged up the certitude that this ordeal had been placed upon me by malevolent Cerulean powers who were gazing down with amused interest and laying bets as to whether I would endure or simply shake down into a blob of mindless protoplasm. We ground up a steep incline, passing a file of peasants, two of whom were carrying a white box between them. The road was no more than two ruts with a high, grassy crown between them. We hurtled over a rise and dipped into a muddy hollow where a stream trickled down toward the lake.

"*Carajo!*" Alfonso observed as the car slowed sickeningly and shuddered to a stop quartering the gelatinous crossing. He shifted into low gear, pressed the gas pedal to the floor, and let out the clutch abruptly. The right wheel spun, of course, splattering the leaves behind us with mud and stones. He tried again, and still again, more violently and more fruitlessly each time. The car tilted slowly and settled on its frame as the rear wheel dug an oozing nest in the mud.

"We are stuck," Alfonso announced. I sighed.

"I could try pushing," I mumbled. Alfonso looked at me judiciously.

"I'll do the pushing," he decided, "and you drive. But first we'll have to get something under that wheel."

We stripped off our shoes and socks, rolled up our pant legs, and stepped out into the cold water. My feet sank down, and mud squirted up between my toes. It made a sucking noise with each painful step. I, Sisyphus, scrabbled dimly for rocks and branches, and wedged them under the offending wheel. I climbed into the driver's seat, exhausted, and started the motor. As Alfonso puffed and grunted behind the car, I released the clutch gently, tenderly. Traction held for a moment, tugged at the car, and I hopefully fed the motor a bit more gas. The rear wheel whinnied, dug up the branches and stones we had fed it so carefully, and flung them merrily backward onto the bank. I tried rocking it out. The wheel slithered irresponsibly in each direction without budging the car.

"Wait a minute, Frank," Alfonso called. "We have some help coming." In the rear view mirror I saw the people with the box toiling over the rise. Alfonso walked barefoot to meet them. I pulled my socks and shoes over my muddy feet and thought about vomiting out the window, but settled for closing my eyes instead.

"Move over," Alfonso told me. "They're going to push us out."

As I eased into my own seat, a man opened the right hand door and deposited the white box in my lap.

"Afterwards, we'll give them a ride as far as the cemetery," Alfonso told me. "It will be good to have the extra weight in the car. Besides, we might get stuck again between here and there."

I stared numbly down at the box. Alfonso put the car in gear, and the wheel whined as the men grunted and strained at the back and sides. We lurched forward with a sucking noise and slammed to a stop on dry ground. Two women and a man climbed into the back seat, another man crowded in beside me, and a young boy mounted the running board. None of them spoke. The man sitting beside me placed a hand on top of the coffin and stared impassively through the windshield. A faint, disagreeable odor seeped into my nostrils. It was hot, and droplets of perspiration were standing out on my forehead again, but I couldn't move to brush them away.

We roared and scraped our way upward interminably. At one point the trees and ground fell away sharply on the right hand side toward the lake, and we jerked spasmodically along within inches of the edge of the declivity. I noted with curiosity that, despite Alfonso's erratic behaviour at the wheel, I felt no alarm. My instinct of self-preservation was dormant or short-circuited; it made no difference to me whether we held to the road or plunged over the edge. The coffin in my lap might just as well have been an orange crate stuffed with old telephone directories.

We finally reached the cemetery. Our passengers got out, and the man beside me relieved me of the coffin. Alfonso pulled a bill out of his wallet and gave it to one of the men. When the party had filed through the gate, I leaned out the open door and vomited again into the road.

"You know, Frank," Alfonso's tone was sympathetic, "I think we'd better turn back." I nodded without speaking.

"Why don't you lie down in the back seat?" he suggested. I pulled myself out, avoiding the puddle soaking into the dust already covered with flies, and crawled into the back of the car. I remember little about the drive back, except that it seemed to last forever.

I seem to recall Alfonso and Isabel helping me into the spare bedroom in their house, and I remember submitting to a spoonful of vile, sweet-smelling medicine. I plucked at buttons with nerveless fingers and protested that my feet were muddy, but I slid between the clean sheets nevertheless and plunged headlong into the abyss of sleep.

December 11, 1931
A few minutes ago, Isabel sat with me while I sipped a cup of broth she made for me. I still haven't tried solid food,

106

but I'm beginning to feel a bit hungry: a welcome sign. I asked her to forgive me for the trouble I've been causing everyone in the household, and most of all herself.

"Don't think about it, Frank," she smiled. "You were terribly sick. During the first two days, Alfonso was worried that you might not live."

I was startled. Death is an event that happens to other people, never to one's self.

"Was it really that serious?" I asked.

She nodded.

"You were delirious the first night, and I couldn't get you to take your medicine."

"You sat up with me?"

"Yes. I had to wake Alfonso, though, to pry your jaws open and make you swallow it." She grinned. "He has an excellent record for saving patients, and he didn't want you to spoil it."

"I would have hated to do that," I agreed. "You're a wonderful nurse, Isabel. Thank you."

She took my empty cup and set it on the night stand.

"I've had practice with the children's illnesses." Her features gathered into an expression of sorrow. "Some months ago we lost a baby boy. He was three months old. Pneumonia."

I murmured something sympathetic.

"It was terrible, but I think Alfonso suffered even more that I did at being unable to save him."

That helped clarify something about her that has puzzled me. She has two healthy, noisy children to occupy her time, all the comforts and help she could wish for in her home, and a respected position in the community as the wife of a successful doctor, yet I've noticed a grave set to her features at times, a shadow behind her eyes that seems to say: "Yes, I have known happiness, but no longer."

Doubtless, it's a tragic thing to watch your own child die, but does that alone explain the sadness? And sometimes she seems to forget, becomes vibrant in the give and take of conversation. I think she feels hemmed in here in this miserable village and needs a much wider field of action to display her full range of being. She seems to have resigned herself to living out the rest of her life in Santa Ana, to acting out the limited roles of doctor's wife, exemplary mother and devout Christian.

What would I be if I didn't carry the conventional labels of wife and mother stamped on my forehead? In the morning when I call the children down to breakfast, my voice is resonant with motherhood. In the evening when I welcome Paul home from the office, I hear myself speaking in sticky-sweet tones: the brave little heroine in a television household drama.

Paul loves his labels (Bureaucrat, Husband, Father) and irritates me with his posturing in the various roles. Yet I find myself responding automatically to him from my own set roles as Understanding Wife; Patient, Forebearing Wife or Wife and Mother of His Children. It's sickening. Who is Paul and who is Carmen? What on earth would they have to say to each other if they set their labels aside?

After all these years, would it still be possible for me to invent a real Carmen? Could I create a genuine person who occupied space self-assuredly and was capable of first-hand experience, authentic reactions? Or shall I continue to echo down an empty corridor where there are only closed doors with neatly-lettered signs painted on them? Carmen existed once; where did she go? Did she dissipate and vanish behind her masks and roles and labels? What ever happened to Mother? Did husbands and children drain us both of our substance and leave only an empty shell?

...This afternoon when she brings refreshments, I'll take her on a tour of the Ile de la Cité. Let's see. Start with the Conciergerie: dark, cold stairways and vaulted ceilings where the French nobility awaited their last ride in the tumbrils. Marie Antoinette's cell? There was an inside balcony where the guards kept watch, and a door leading directly into the tiny chapel. Yes.

Then, around the corner to the Prefecture, point out the wall clock, and we'll visit the Sainte Chapelle. I've forgotten the lower floor. Never mind. Concentrate on the stained glass on the floor above; the delicate, soaring pillars that support the expanse of glass; the fine stone tableaux in the portal. An afternoon sun, perhaps, streaming through the primitive, storytelling squares.

Then (I'll save Notre Dame for another time) we'll stroll toward the Pont Neuf, down the stairs behind the statue of the *Vert Galant,* and around the park at the point of the island. Watch barges chugging upstream, throw rocks in the Seine, etc., etc....

December 12, 1931

Virgil came by this afternoon with my belongings and the news that he had to go to Guatemala for some weeks. He had the distracted air of an overworked businessman.

"I got a letter from my bishop," he explained. "He wants me to help a newcomer establish a mission in Chichicastenango. If you decide to leave before I get back, why don't you stop through there on your way to Mexico? They say it's an interesting little place."

I had an unexpected sinking feeling when he mentioned my leaving Santa Ana. A ridiculous reaction, considering I've accomplished little other than to serve as host to hordes of microscopic fauna and as target for a knife-wielding drunk since my arrival.

"In the meantime," he continued, "you'd be doing me a favor if you moved back into my place whenever you feel up to it. I'd feel more comfortable if someone were living there."

I accepted his offer and promised to leave the key with the Rojas' when I left.

"Sit down and talk for a while, Virgil," I urged him. "You've been so busy with your affairs and I with being an invalid that we haven't really had a chance to get reacquainted."

"Sure." He draped himself in the chair, scratched his head, and grinned. "We've had enough time, Frank, but we Anglo-Saxons are pretty reticent people."

"It wasn't like that when we were kids," I protested. "Remember that summer in the Sierras? As I recall, we did a lot of talking around the fire at night."

"I've often remembered that trip," he nodded.

"I never asked you what you did with your share of the money. I bought a boat passage to Paris with mine and got a foothold there."

"Let's see. I returned to the University that fall and went on with my studies...Of course, I remember!" he interrupted himself. "I bought a dozen yearlings and put them out to pasture on my Dad's farm. They were pretty little Herefords."

"I should have done something practical myself," I mused. "How did you happen to become a missionary, Virgil? As I remember, you didn't display any metaphysical yearnings that summer in the mountains.

He frowned down at the floor and shook his head slowly.

"As they say down here, it was pure fate. In my junior year, I fell head over heels for a girl named Joan. Her father was an Adventist minister. I taught Sunday school there and sat through all his sermons in order to be close to Joan. In my last year I made up my mind to become a missionary."

He paused and shrugged perplexedly.

"Thinking about it now, I'm not sure how much of it was sincere and how much was just the notion of impressing Joan and her folks."

"What happened?"

Virgil blushed and shook his head again.

"You're gonna laugh, Frank. "Two months before I took my Divinity degree, she ran off with another student at the seminary. They live in Kansas City now.

"So what did I do?" His gesture bespoke resignation. "I had to prove she wasn't all that important, so I went ahead just like I'd planned and became a missionary." He grinned sheepishly. "And here I am, with my satchel and pills and congregation, and without Joan."

He turned serious.

"Don't think I'm complaining, Frank. My work here, the Bible, have given me something I probably would never have found any other way."

Yesterday — my last day of convalescence at the Rojas' home — I persuaded Isabel to tell me something about her childhood.

"I was the only girl in the family for a good many years," she said, "and since my three brothers would have nothing to do with dolls and tea parties, I had to play boys' games or keep to myself. I tried to compete with the boys, but I finally learned it was no use, and I became a bookworm instead."

"What does a girl do in Santa Ana before she's married?"

"It's a standarized ritual. You stay at home, mostly, being as remote and mysterious as you can. You're allowed to go to suitable dances and parties, provided they are chaperoned, of course. And in the evenings you can stroll around the park with several giggling girl friends, pretending not to notice the boys who are all strolling in the opposite direction."

And after you finished school?" I insisted.

She pursed her lips adorably and looked thoughtful.

"We all studied piano until we could play 'For Elisa,' several Chopin Nocturnes, and the first movement of 'The Moonlight Sonata.' Learning to crochet was also obligatory. Our mothers taught us to prepare four or five exquisite dishes, but not a single, plain everyday dish. And we learned to carry ourselves as though we were so fragile we couldn't possibly pick up a pin.

"Our future husbands found all of this irresistible, until after they were married. Then they began to realize that we weren't really mysterious, merely insipid. They, of course,

111

had been raised differently, in an active, masculine world." She smiled wryly. "How do those things work in Oregon?"

I gave her a brief rundown on the problems of being a Protestant minister's son in a small town.

"I felt tragic and misunderstood," Isabel laid a hand on her cheek, gazed soulfully at the ceiling, and then flashed an impish grin. "After reading *The Lady of the Camellias*, I modelled myself after her and wandered about the house feeling brave and tuberculous. Why is one such an idiot, Frank?"

"Insecurity, I suppose."

She gazed at me musingly.

"Sometimes I'm not certain that I ever did set aside the Lady of the Camellias. I know it's stupid, but once in a while I still find myself gesturing or posing as I used to imagine she did."

She gestured impatiently.

"I watch Carmen growing up here, and I feel real anguish to see her heading straight into the trap, the same net of insipid, conventional behavior that snared me. It's Santa Ana itself that insists on all women acting in conformity to the one pattern. And Alfredo? If he stays here long enough, he'll learn to drink, to be a small town Don Juan, to think that next season's coffee price is the most important thing in the world."

She shuddered with distaste.

"I have to do something — anything — to get the children away from this environment. I must give them what I never had: the opportunity to choose their own way of life."

Alfredo returned after two years in the States, and it's just as though he'd never been away. And I? What offering have I to lay on her grave but the thorns of failure?

Are you sure that's the right thing to do, Isabel?" I asked. "I don't think Carmen could find a better example anywhere to model herself on than you."

She blushed and looked down at the floor. I couldn't find any words, and the two of us fell silent until Alfonso finished with his last patient and bustled out of his clinic a few moments later.

We set up the chess pieces and started to play almost without speaking. We are tied in a tournament that has gone on for a number of days now. His unorthorodox attack no longer disconcerts me. He's a better natural player than I am, but he relies entirely on intuition, whereas I have read some of the books. Besides, I'm trying harder now than I did at first. I'm beginning to find his constant, driving will to win irritating.

Alfonso hurls himself at everything with the same blind confidence that he displays behind the wheel of an automobile. He has a direct, blunt way of saying exactly what he thinks; there's no tact or sensibility to him at all. But this frankness is so integral a part of his character that it totally disarms his victims. You can't really resent him when he takes some skin off you; you can only shrug and tell yourself:

"He can't help it; that's just the way he is."

I can visualize him as a successful Wall Street broker or captain of industry, if there are any left these days. He dominates any group he's in by virtue of sheer vitality. It's not that he's a dictatorial type, simply that he's a person with no inner contradictions or doubts: a man who is absolutely convinced that his point of view is the only right one, merely because it is the one he happens to hold.

I can't understand how Isabel came to marry him; the two are diametrical opposites. Or perhaps I can. Isabel was the prettiest girl in Santa Ana, so Alfonso chose her. It must have been as uncomplicated as that, and nobody, starting with Isabel herself, had the energy or determination to stand betwen him and his objective.

Had I been living here at the time, had I been Alfonso's rival, would I have won out over him?

Probably not. I was as unsure of myself at that time as he was cocksure. After a few, faint-hearted attempts, I suppose I would have stepped aside and let him take her from me.

December 17, 1931

What in God's name is happening to me? I have never before been literally beside myself, standing by and watching my puppet body being moved by a force beyond its control. Am I self-hypnotized, going mad? How did it happen?

I had been alone here in Virgil's house all day long with nothing to read and nothing to do. I lay on the bed listening to street noises muffled by tropic heat, thinking drowsily about Santa Ana, its Gothic cathedral with dwarf towers, its slow, organic rhythm that's come to seem as natural and uncomplicated as breathing.

My thoughts turned to Isabel, what she had told me of her childhood in this town, of her marriage and her preoccupations as a mother, of certain, tenuous clues in her conversation which have led me to believe that she knows or suspects that Alfonso has been unfaithful to her. My mind seized on this thought, I remember now, and inspected it carefully. Suddenly, irrationally, I was seized with elation.

"She doesn't love him," I told myself. "She's living out her marriage for the sake of the children. That's the reason for her basic sadness, her resignation."

I was so excited by this idea that I got up and paced the room. No, I thought, I'm imagining things. She has never given any hint that she has even imagined the possibility of another sort of life. She's unhappy in Santa Ana, yes. But her acceptance of unhappiness encloses her acceptance of her marriage, her acceptance of the same life here stretching ahead interminably. And so I argued with myself, yes, and no, and maybe, and stood up and sat down and looked at my watch every ten minutes until it was time to leave.

Alfonso was out on a call as I had hoped he would be, and I was nervous in her presence, sensitized to her smallest

114

gesture, the most infinitesimal nuance of her voice. But she was the same as always, and we sat in the same chairs in the shade of the corridor.

During my convalescence, I had exhausted not only my memories of Paris streets and bridges and museums but also my more superficial recollections of Venice, Florence, Rome and Madrid. So I started talking about the trip I made to Yucatan several years ago when I was living in Mexico. I described Chichen Itza to her: the Palace of the Warriors, the pyramid housing the chamber of the jaguar idol, the huge ball court where players wagered all their possessions and their very lives.

I'll admit that I was talking to hold her attention, to keep her dark eyes fixed unmovingly on my face. I've been playing a dangerous game for some time now: one not entirely exempt from deliberate intent. I have exercised a species of verbal seduction as I led her, figuratively, by the hand through the streets of Paris and other cities. But I swear that what I said this afternoon was unpremeditated. I didn't plan it, didn't even imagine the possibility until it happened, of and by itself.

I led her to the edge of the large *cenote* in Chichen Itza, described the vertical limestone wall, the murky water, and told her how the Mayans had sacrificed virgins there each year. I paused.

"They would have chosen you, Isabel," I blurted suddenly, "because you are beautiful. But I wouldn't have let them. I would have swept you up and taken you away."

I stopped again, my unexpected words echoing in my ears. I think I stopped breathing in the silence that hung between us. But she didn't take her eyes from my face, and I was in deep water again, hurled along by the current. It started as an apology, I think: that I had never met a woman like her, that I found myself obsessed by her image, her words; that here I was, chained to Santa Ana like Prometheus to his rock, with the vultures of love tearing at my insides; that I couldn't bring

115

myself to imagine spending my days and my nights away from her. And I stopped, appalled again at my own words.

She looked away toward the patio fountain, and then she turned back to me.

"I don't know what to say, Frank." There was no reproach in her eyes. "It has been my fault, I know. Too many confidences..."

Her eyes brimmed suddenly, and she leaned forward, took my hand impulsively. Was it a gesture of love? Sympathy? Pity? The question flashed through my mind.

And then — in exactly these words — then she said to me:

"I would have wanted nothing more than to marry a man like you, Frank. Why did you have to come too late?"

December 25, 1931

Every day during the past week when I arrived for the afternoon chess game, the servant told me that Isabel was not at home, that she was off visiting her sister or one or another of her aunts. Invariably, she would arrive when Alfonso and I were halfway through our game, and she would disappear into her room.

Several nights ago, I remained for dinner at Alfonso's invitation, and there was an electric crackling in the air between Isabel and myself. Alfonso, of course, is oblivious to such things, and when he invited me to spend Christmas Eve at their house, I accepted immediately. I was desperate to talk to her under any circumstances.

There have been times this past week when I was sure I was going out of my mind. The night before last I awoke an hour or two after I had gone to bed, and I lay staring wide-eyed at the darkness until dawn lit the window. I've been racking my brain to figure out a way to see her alone, with no servants, friends, or children loitering about. There is absolutely no way to hold a private conversation in this miserable village unless both parties agree to meet under a coffee tree somewhere on a hillside. I even thought of going to morning Mass, but she's been avoiding me deliberately, and, undoubtedly, she would have bolted like a startled deer had I shown up at the church.

I arrived at the Rojas' last evening determined to corner her, if only for five minutes. The house was buzzing with friends and members of the family drifting in with holiday greetings, milling about, and eventually departing for the next stop on the Christmas rounds. Children ran screaming around the corridor and exploded firecrackers deafeningly in the patio.

Isabel greeted me formally when I entered, but there was a hint of hidden mirth in her eyes as we shook hands.

"Merry Christmas, Frank. I'm so glad you could come."

There were people all around us and a hubbub of intermingled conversations.

"Isabel, I have to talk to you."

She shook her head almost imperceptively and guided me firmly to where Alfonso was standing with a group of his friends. She slipped away as Alfonso clapped me on the shoulder and introduced me around the circle, and I lost sight of her. I accepted a glass of tomato juice from the servant (tomato juice on Christmas Eve, for God's sake!) and listened with one ear to the conversation. The men were discussing the recent incident in Ahuachapan in which a mass of discontented peasants had surrounded the National Guard fortress and threatened to storm it with bare hands and *machetes*.

"The commander should be court-martialed for cowardice," a glowering coffee baron rapped. "He should have opened up with machine-guns and taught them a needed lesson. This country will go to the devil if Martínez doesn't put an end to all this insolence and anarchy."

I peered past the circle to catch occasional glimpses of Isabel as she moved from group to group making sure everyone was supplied with drinks. She was watching me, too, out of the corner of her eye, and when I made an abortive move toward her, she darted behind a phalanx of fat ladies and settled down out of reach. She lurked behind the mountainous matrons until it was time for us to set off on foot for midnight Mass, and all the way she travelled in convoy, with one of them on either side of her. I dropped behind and was lured out of my obsession for some moments by the luminous stars that seemed to dangle in the sky just beyond my reach.

In the church, jammed shoulder to shoulder with strangers, immersed in a warm broth of perfume, perspiration and the odor of candlewax, my ear registered the meaningless chants and I remembered the cold, drizzly Christmases of Oregon and the boundless love I had once upon a time felt for the Infant Jesus. Then I started thinking of Isabel, who had eluded me once again. I didn't see her until the Mass was over. I posted myself in the thronged shadows outside the main door and executed a perfectly-timed flank attack as she paused, blinking, to adjust her eyes to the darkness.

"You've been dodging me for days," I accused her as I hurried her into the deeper darkness. "If I don't get a chance to talk to you, I'll explode."

She placed a petitioning hand on my arm.

"I've been thinking about it, Frank. This can't go on any longer. You'll have to leave Santa Ana as soon as you can."

I stared down at the dim oval of her face, choked back the impulsive answer that rose in my throat.

"I have to talk to you alone, Isabel. You can't end this by simply slamming the door in my face. You wouldn't do that to a beggar."

She shook her head stubbornly.

"There's nothing for us to talk about, Frank. You'll have to go."

I gripped her arm and swung her around to face me.

"I'm not going to leave Santa Ana until I've had a chance to have my say, Isabel. And I'll give you no peace until I do see you. That's a promise."

She looked up at me, startled, and was about to reply when one of her maiden aunts caught up with us, linked her arm in Isabel's, and started chattering idiotically about the dresses that had attended Mass. I said goodnight at the next corner, returned to Virgil's, and went to bed.

Merry Christmas, Frank!

December 29,1931

Dammit! She's gone to San Salvador "to nurse her sister, Maruca," according to Alfonso. I've written her a letter, and I'll send another tomorrow, and another the day after that. Will she read them? Of course she will!

January 8, 1932

She wrote me! She has been reading them! Begs me to stop writing her. She'll be back tomorrow. I wonder...

January 10, 1932

She's mine! Mine! Mine! I was right: she loves me, not Alfonso! I'm giddy; can't hold the pen steady; can't think. And it's time to think and act now. The world has started revolving again, and at last it's time to act.

Projects? I have dozens of them! I'll make her happy; that's the principal one, the only important one.

She came to me early this morning instead of going to Mass. She slipped away from her barred and bolted tower and knocked on my door just as I finished shaving, before I even had a shirt on. She knocked lightly on the door and slipped inside like a frightened bird when I opened it.

"Frank," she spoke hurriedly, breathlessly, before I could so much as open my mouth, "I've come as you asked, but you'll have to promise you'll leave today — this afternoon."

I caught at her hand, but she dodged and put the table between us.

"Please sit down over on the bed," she ordered severely. She herself sat down behind the table and folded her hands like a schoolmarm taking recitation.

119

"You see, I'm not slamming the door on you; I've come to hear what you have to say."

I saw she was as nervous as a squirrel, and I started talking to her gently, soothing her. What did I say? I can't remember; I wasn't taking note of my own words. Something to the effect that I'd never met anyone for whom I had felt such an immense and immediate attraction, so close a bond of identical enthusiasms and interests. That because of that link between the two of us, I knew directly, intuitively, that she wasn't happy, couldn't be happy, here in Santa Ana, married to someone who didn't share her same tastes, her sensitivity.

She shook her head slightly, never removing her eyes from my face; but her hands were resting quietly on the table now.

"Don't deny it, Isabel. You can't deny it!" I moved to the table and sat down across from her. "You made a mistake when you married Alfonso. It wasn't your fault. You were young, and all you knew of the world was Santa Ana. But it's time now to correct it. You can't throw your whole life away because of one error."

I took her hands in mine. She closed her eyes for a moment and then looked at me again. Her voice was uneven when she spoke.

"No, Frank. I chose Alfonso, Santa Ana, this life that I have. I knew he and I were different, but I accepted that before I married him. It's just that you came along and swept me off balance for a moment."

She freed her hands and stood up.

"That couldn't have happened if you still loved Alfonso. You don't. But I love you, Isabel. I need you."

The time for talking was over, and the table was no longer between us. She struggled when I took her in my arms and kissed her.

"No!" she gasped. "Please, Frank! I have to leave."

"Isabel! I love you, Isabel." I twined my fingers in the jet black hair at the nape of her neck and kissed her again: lips, cheek, the line of her jaw, her neck, her lips again. Her

120

trembling tenseness escaped at last with a sigh, and she crumpled against me, responded on tiptoe, eyes tightly closed.

We strained toward each other for a long moment: her soft, smooth body, her breasts, pressing against me, burning into me through her thin summer dress. When I led her to the bed, she came docilely, sweetly.

And afterwards, after the eager giving, the selfish taking, the high, soaring ecstasy, running her hands lightly over my back, my shoulders, she repeated softly, memorizing the phrase:

"Frank, I love you. I love you."

Why did she leave me this diary, this yellowing notebook with its hasty, inked scrawlings now faded after thirty years? The pages are dog-eared, worn with much handling and rereading. What moved her, after holding the secret all these years, to pass this to me wordlessly, with no explanation, like a sudden slap in the face from the other side of the grave?

January 13, 1931

Everything is arranged. The boat leaves from La Libertad on the 19th. I learned in San Salvador, after cabling my bank and making the reservations, that there'll be a slight passport problem. Isabel and the children will have to leave for another "visit to Maruca" the day after tomorrow to get that straightened out. Less than a week, and we'll be on our way to Paris. She's coming to me this afternoon, and I'll surprise her with the news...

"Hi!" Eugenia walks into the bedroom. "I see you're reading the diary."

"Yes." She leans down and we kiss each other. "I read it through last night in one sitting. Now I'm going through it again more slowly. Why don't you spend the night here, Eugenia. I want to talk to you."

Chapter Fourteen

Alfredo and Eduardo are seated by the coffee table in the corridor. Eugenia and I take our usual places, and María comes padding from the kitchen with the tray of drinks. The scene is reassuringly familiar. Alfredo serves himself a double Scotch (Dad was right; he's started in again) and fixes two weaker ones for Eugenia and myself. Eduardo removes the cap from his soft drink; it's been years since he touched liquor.

I remember the afternoon of the storm. An enormous, dark cloud swallowed the sun while Alicia and I were playing in the patio. Aunt Rosa sent us to look for Eduardo.

"He's bound to be in the *Aquí me quedo*," she told us, "Hurry up, because it's going to rain."

The wind caught us, whipped at our clothing, before we reached the *cantina*. It spat leaves and handfuls of sand at us, bent the trees until they creaked and tossed their branches in desperation. A blackbird whipped frantically across the sky, hunting its nest. The first, fat drops came down, drumming hollowly on the sidewalk.

Eduardo is leaning back in a corner, smelling of vomit and *aguardiente*. We shake him, raise him protesting to his feet, steer him toward the door. A prostitute in a shocking pink dress screams an insult at him and empties her beer glass over his head. From the street we can hear her cursing all the men in the world and hurling glasses against the wall.

The purple, blue, black cloud hangs above us menacingly and then splits open. The street springs alive with puddles and rivulets splotched by the driving droplets. Thick streams of water gush from the roofs and splatter on the sidewalk, and the earth gives off the odor of rotting leaves.

Eduardo comes to life; I look up at him. A bolt of lightning fills the world with its livid hammer-blow; the Eduardo of that instant remains etched in my mind: head thrown back, mouth gaping, howling with stupid laughter.

"Colonel Gutiérrez finally died," Alfredo announces over the rim of his glass. "They'll be bringing the body over to the Guard barracks any time now."

"I know. Dr. Selva brought us the news a little while ago. Where's Ana?"

"She couldn't come. Marcelita has a bad cough. The funeral is going to be terrific. Carlos Samayoa has ordered all businesses to close tomorrow so everyone can go."

"Where's Alfonso?" Eduardo interrupts.

"He went off to play billiards with Dr. Selva, but he should be back soon."

"Good!" Eduardo puts his feet up on the coffee table. "That will be good for him. He's been overwhelmed by all this."

"We all have," Eugenia sighs. "This house is going to be a cemetery when you leave, Carmen."

"And he's asked for the military band from San Salvador. He wants it to be a funeral fit for a general."

"Ah, Carlos!" Eduardo shakes his head. "As mayor, he's even worse than Dicky Durán was. Has the same mania for cutting down all the trees in town. Palm Avenue was the last shady street in town, and what does Carlos do? Down with the trees! And he has it widened to make it look like Canal Street."

"No. Dicky was worse," Alfredo contradicts him. "Did you go to his party last month?" Eduardo grins and nods affirmatively. Alfredo turns to me. "It was in honor of Nena Hernández and her husband while they were here on vacation."

"Nena told me how surprised she was when Dicky arranged the party for them," Eugenia offers. "They've never been particularly close friends."

"Ah-h-h! It was because her husband's a major in the Marine Corps, that's why," Alfredo shrugs. "You should have been here, Carmen; it was a real Marx brothers comedy. Three hundred guests, at least. When Nena and Joe got out of the car, Dicky fired off a five-round salute with his cannon, and then the marimba band struck up the Marine hymn. You know, the one that goes: 'From the halls of Montezuma to the shores of someplace or other.'"

"Honestly?" Eugenia giggles.

"Ask Eduardo if it isn't so. Then Dicky presented Joe all around as a hero of the war in Viet Nam. I was impressed until Nena told me that Joe had never been near Viet Nam. He has a desk job in the Pentagon. Then Dicky herded us into the living room, showed us his medals again, and told Joe how he'd been appointed a colonel in the American army during the Second World War."

"I didn't know about that."

"Of course not! He made it all up. He bought the medals in a pawn shop in the States."

"What do they think about that at the American Embassy?" I ask.

"They don't care. Dicky plays golf with the Ambassador, tells him jokes, and informs him about the dangerous subversives here in Santa Ana. The Ambassador thinks he's a great guy."

"He's disgusting," Eduardo says emphatically. "There's nothing he won't do to get in good with the Americans. I was at a dinner he gave for the Ambassador, and we ate lobster which he said he'd flown down alive from Maine. Can you imagine that!"

"Probably another of his lies," Eugenia suggests.

"No, he's capable of an idiocy like that," Alfredo disagrees, "but have you ever seen the shacks his workers live in on the finca? They have to walk half a mile for water. He's built a brick chapel for them, though, and he has Father Antonio come out once a month to preach conformity to them."

"But didn't he build a school for the children?" I ask.

"There's an old shed with a dirt floor. He says it's the state's business to build schools."

"Nothing has happened in this country for the past thirty years," I complain. "Time wears on, but everything stays the same."

125

"And nothing will change until there's a revolution and people like Dicky are run out of the country," Alfredo flashes.

"No, Alfredo." Eduardo pats his pockets for cigarets. "I thought the way you do when I was young. Hooray for the Revolution! and all that. But reality isn't that simple. It isn't white or black; it's gray. Things change slowly. Another general slaughter won't solve El Salvador's problems."

"The Duráns fly lobsters in from Maine; more than half the children in the country live in filth and misery and never learn to read, and you recommend patience!" Alfredo exclaims.

"The policies of this government are sound," Eduardo replies calmly. "I sit on the Appropriations Committee, and I know we are spending as much as the country can afford on education, social welfare and health."

"How much do you spend on the army?" Alfredo retorts hotly. "And how much goes to line the pockets of the president and his ministers?"

"It's the government's job to preserve order and prevent anarchy, and we need an army," Eduardo says stubbornly. "I know there are kickbacks on construction contracts, but there's bound to be corruption in every poor country, and we are getting schools and housing projects built in spite of that. You've seen them."

"Sure," Alfredo mocks. "Our famous general built highways — the best highway system in Central America — and now he's sitting in the Miami Beach hotel he bought with his graft. We've been marching colonels through the presidential palace ever since then. They're all the same."

I intervene before the two of them lose their tempers entirely.

"Do you remember Frank Wolff, Eduardo?"

"What's gotten into you about Frank Wolff?" Alfredo asks irritably. Eugenia flashes me a panic-stricken glance.

"Of course I remember him," Eduardo replies. "He used to come here and play chess with your Dad, didn't he? I remember I drove him and that American missionary out to

126

Izalco to meet Martí just before the uprising in 1932. I wonder what ever became of him?"

"Did you hear from him after he left Santa Ana?"

"Not a word. He disappeared into thin air one day. He was a timid sort; I think he was scared to death by the uprising."

Dad enters, dragging his feet along the tiles. He nods to Eugenia and Eduardo.

"You!" he frowns at Alfredo, who has hastily pushed his empty glass to the center of the coffee table. "Why didn't you show up this afternoon? You know I needed you."

"I came, but you were asleep," Alfredo answers defensively. "Wasn't I here, Carmen?"

"Why didn't you wait until I woke up?" Dad jerks the rocking chair up to the coffee table and sits down. "And you told Carmen you'd be right back, but you never came. What's your excuse for that?"

Alfredo flushes and doesn't answer. Eduardo nervously clears his throat and crosses his legs. We are immobile in the blue twilight. My gaze takes in the puma skin rug that Alfredo used to wrap around himself, the solid, square Spanish chairs with their blackened leather straps — Mother loved that set — and shifts to Salarrue's tapestry on the wall, the yellow flower vase under it, the mahogany cabinet of the record player.

María appears at my side.

"Shall I serve dinner now?" she asks, and we all breathe again. I lead the way into the dining room and take my seat at Mother's place. I find myself imitating her remembered gestures, her way of tilting her head to one side, as I ladle out the soup. She has gone, but nothing has changed. I sit in her chair, carrying out her role, gazing with her eyes across the table at Dad. She lends them a mixture of sympathy and reproach as they light on Alfredo, sitting in his usual chair with the furtive air of a mischievous child weathering a scolding. Eugenia sits at my place, a little wilted now, but

127

still beautilful with her Grecian profile, almond eyes, dark skin.

Matisse should have painted Eugenia as an indolent odalisque, reclining against pillows in primary colors, cooling herself with a fan of playing cards, while in the background writhes a tangle of green and yellow plastic leaves which Ricardo ordered for her from New Orleans.

"You should read more instead of playing so much canasta," Mother advised her.

"Ay, Isabel," she answers slowly, "you know there aren't any books here. I'd have to go all the way to San Salvador to look for them."

Eduardo is fat now, and gray-haired. Mother's hair was still black; only a few gray streaks glinted in the candlelight as I kissed her cold forehead the last time. She isn't here; that's the only change. But everything is starting to tilt, crumble, slide into the past. This dining room, the corridors, the bedrooms, will slowly take on a barren, disinhabited look. The cut flowers will disappear first, then the vases and the crocheted doilies, then the pictures from the walls. Her home, her world, will crumble into nothingness along with her, and none of us can stop it. In three months or a year the house will be different, unrecognizable, and Dad, if he is still alive, will be unaware of all the small differences that have led to the change; he will feel only that the house is empty and dank now that she has gone.

How old Dad looks, the lines of his face accentuated by the candlelight. When we were young, Alfredo and I weren't permitted to speak at the table without permission. After dinner he would play with us in the patio, tell us the story of how Uncle Coyote burned his tail, or recite long passages out of *Don Quixote* from memory. Once in a while he would tell about the long marches through Nicaraguan jungle when he was fighting with Sandino's guerrillas.

His expression has changed now that Mother is gone. His life work is finished, and he has nothing to do with his time except play billiards, quarrel with Alfredo, or sit in his rocking chair. He hasn't fully grasped that yet. When he does, he will die of the knowledge.

The candles flicker and bend before a puff of air from the open window. The golden light is thrown back in wavering highlights from her silver, her porcelain, the snowy sheen of her damask tablecloth as we reverently spoon our soup.

"I nearly forgot," Alfredo addresses me. "I ran into Toña Figueroa today, and she asked me to say hello."

"How is she?" Toña and I were classmates in Hectór's school. She would have been elected Santa Ana's coffee queen the year we graduated if she hadn't come from a middle-class family. "Is that idiot, Meme, still ashamed to be seen with her?"

"He never takes her to parties, but she comes into town to shop once a week. I met her coming out of Turco Sadid's."

"Meme's not a bad sort," Eugenia defends her brother-in-law. "He's just old-fashioned. He needn't have married her, you know; he could have just set her up in a house like the other pretty *mengala* girls."

"He's an imbecile, and there's no cure for that!" Eduardo lays down his spoon and glares at Eugenia. Eduardo married a middle-class girl too when he was still a hopeless drunk. We all love her because she has always been so patient and self-sacrificing with him. But Eduardo always took her to the Casino and everywhere, and she was gradually accepted. Now even Eugenia has forgotten her background, but Eduardo hasn't.

"How is Marcelita today?" Dad asks Alfredo while I serve the main course.

"She has a bad cough. I wish you'd come and look at her."

"There's a lot of whooping cough going around," Eugenia warns. "You'd better keep her away from the other children."

"Ana tries to," Alfredo grins, "but she can't control that pirate gang, especially now that school is out. They're driving us both crazy, and she can't even scare them with Filiberta any more. Remember, Carmen?"

"You get a move on, or I'll call Filiberta," Cata used to warn us when we dawdled taking our baths. What does Filiberta do for a living? Carmen Bomba sold lottery tickets and his freehand verses. He used to stop outside the window when I was practicing and ask me to play "For Elise" for him. Deaf'n Dumb Mercedes would come around dressed in baggy Indian pants, straw hat jammed down to his eyebrows, and hold out the little slip of paper on which was scrawled: "Please help this poor deaf-mute." How does Filiberta live? She doesn't beg. She drags herself along the street with spastic jerks, barefoot, bulging-eyed, propping herself with her cane. When we saw her coming at a distance, we used to scream in chorus:

"Old Filiberta, Hooty-Owl, Nanny-Goat!" and we would dash around the corner with our hearts in our throats while she screeched at us and shook her cane unsteadily.

Filiberta hasn't changed either, except that her hair is white now. I passed by her yesterday as a handful of children screamed the same refrain and scattered out of reach of her cane, and I thought I saw, behind the spastic convulsions twisting her features, a secret delight at playing the dreaded, wicked witch for the children of Santa Ana.

"Take good care of her," Dad seconds Eugenia's warning. "Bronchitis can be dangerous in a child of that age. Neto's illness started just that way, and he was gone within three days."

"Niña Carmen, did you remember your kerchief?"

I hold it up for Cata's inspection as we enter the hospital.

"And don't you go telling your mother about this; she mightn't like it. But you'll see: there's nothing as miraculous as the new souls in Purgatory."

"I don't want to go, Cata. I'm afraid."

"Don't you be silly. It's for your little brother."

The corridor is crowded with people awaiting their turn at the charity clinic: a woman with a swollen, elephantine leg; a mother holding a rachitic child whose head lolls to one side and whose mouth hangs open. The air is heavy with the odor of medicines and sickness. Cata hustles me down the passageway past a stretcher bearing a man with a heavy bandage around his head and over one eye.

"Uff!" Cata shudders. "God save me from ever entering this place. There aren't many who come out alive. My brother, Carlos, says you just lie around and the nurses don't pay a bit of attention to you."

We enter through the low door, and flies buzz up from the gray sheets covering four long bundles on the floor. We kneel before the crucifix on the wall, and the buzzing diminishes as the flies alight once more. Cata hands me the missal. She can't read.

"I can't find the page, Cata. Can't we just say an Ave Maria?"

"If you don't find it, we'll pray a whole rosary," she threatens.

But Neto died anyway.

Afterwards, when Mother shut herself up in the bedroom, Cata gave free rein to her religiosity. Every night after dinner she called Alfredo and me to the kitchen, made us read the *novenas* aloud, and then subjected us to her interminable, free-style versions of the lives of the saints. Angela, on the other hand, was almost pure Indian and not so good a Catholic. She would iron until Cata finished with us. Then she would pour herself a cup of coffee, sit down with her legs spread apart and her elbows on the table, and grin at us while we clamored for her to tell us about the *Siguanaba*.

"Ah, I'm tired of that. You always ask me for that one," she protests. But she gathers me into her lap while Alfredo settles down on the floor, and she begins:

"The *Siguanaba* is tall and beautiful with long, black hair..."

131

"It reaches clear to her knees," Alfredo interrupts.

"She stole another woman's husband, and Tlaloc condemned her to wander by the river forever, never speaking to a soul. She comes out at night and hides beside the path that follows the edge of the river, waiting for a man to come riding by in the darkness. When a lone rider comes along, she springs up behind him on the horse and wraps her arms about him with a terrible scream. The man loses his mind at her touch: he can't remember his name, or where he came from, or where he was going. He can't remember anything after that but the terrible scream and the cold arms clutching him in the darkness."

We shiver delightedly.

"And she caught your cousin that way, didn't she?"

"Yes," Angela nods and her gold tooth flashes. "Poor Pedro has been crazy ever since."

"It was his own fault," Cata sniffs as she unbraids her hair. "He turned Protestant, and God doesn't watch over Protestants."

"He only had a slight cold," Dad toys with the silverware, and his eyes focus beyond me, "but that weakened him, and he caught pneumonia."

Strange that Dad should be talking about Neto's death. There was always an unspoken agreement among us to avoid any mention of Neto in his presence.

"There were no antibiotics in those days," he sighs. "There wasn't a thing I could do."

Angela finishes drying him after his bath.

"All right," she says. "You can hold him while I go and bring the diapers." He gurgles and catches at my nose. I dance him around the room to make him laugh, carry him to the window to watch the squad of Guards marching out of the barracks across the street. It was open. Was there a draft?

132

Was I...?

"My God!" Paul snaps. "James is only six months old, and you've already had two Caesarians. Be sensible."

"But, Paul, it's a crime."

"That's ridiculous! It's just a matter of scraping away some tissue."

He doesn't speak for three days, floods the house with his tense, nerve-rasping anger and the Doctor looks up from my card, light glinting off his glasses like Father Antonio, his face pale, thin-lipped, expressionless. He taps the card.

"We may as well get it over with right away, Mrs. Pierson."

Mother never knew. She couldn't have suspected.

"You're pale, Carmen," Eugenia peers at me. "What's the matter?"

"Nothing." I start spooning out the dessert.

"*Icaco* sauce!" Alfredo exclaims. "Remember how crazy Mother was about *icacos*?"

"And mangos," Eugenia laughs. "When Maruca and I were kids, we used to hide in the bathroom and eat them so she wouldn't take them away from us."

"She was always happy, always so good-humored and smiling," Alfredo recalls.

"No, she wasn't," Dad contradicts him. "Your mother was a quiet woman — serious and quiet."

"How do you remember her, Eduardo?" I ask.

"Let's see. She was very conservative when she was young, but it's curious: the older she got, the more she turned to the left. She had a very generous heart."

All of us saw her differently, including Frank. The six blind men and the elephant. In the coffin with her eyes closed, the tension of life absent from her features; vibrant at the edge of the *cenote* with the proud air of a Mayan princess;

133

laughter bubbling from her throat as she packed for a trip; grave and intent — my most detailed memory now — as we stroll side by side along the corridor, her keys jingling at her waist.

"It's so hot," Eugenia fans herself with her napkin. "I thought we were going to get some rain."

"Why don't we go to the patio?" I suggest, as she always did when dinner was over. I touch my hair with her gesture, rise, and lead the others out. Dad's chair scrapes heavily across the tiles.

"I'm going to bed," he announces. "I'll come by tomorrow to see Marcelita," he tells Alfredo. He drags his feet down the corridor toward his room, his arms swinging loosely like pendulums. He shouldn't be left alone; I'll have to speak to Alfredo.

We settle in the chairs, and the desultory conversation begins. I close my eyes and listen to the voices, the phrases punctuated by the plop of insect bodies striking against the light bulbs in the corridor.

Chapter Fifteen

The sound of voices, of automobiles arriving at Colonel Gutierrez's wake, drifts across the rooftop into the patio. Eduardo and Alfredo have left, lured by the sociability across the street. The jasmine is blossoming tonight, and its heavy perfume surrounds us.

"How did you learn about Mother and Frank?" I ask Eugenia.

"It was before Frank disappeared — before the uprising. I was at Mass with her one morning, and I asked her why she didn't take communion."

"'I can't,' she told me. After Mass we went to Calvario park to talk. 'I don't know what to do,' she said. 'I've fallen in love with Frank.' And she told me the whole story."

Eugenia lays a supplicating hand on my arm.

"You must try to understand her, Carmen. I know how hard it is for you. But I was at her side the whole time, and I know how much she suffered. There were so many things. When she was carrying Neto she found out Alfonso was having an affair with another woman. Until then, I know, she loved him very much. When the baby was born she turned all her love, all her attention, towards it. But then Neto died, and I think something gave way inside her. Frank came along just a little while after that, and I'm sure she still hadn't recovered completely. You can't pass judgement on her, Carmen. None of us can.

"And she was proud; don't forget that. Papa Manuel used to tease her; he nick-named her 'the Princess' because of the haughty way she carried herself. I know she tried to forgive Alfonso, but deep down inside I don't think she ever could.

"I'm different," Eugenia shrugs lightly. "When I found out that Ricardo was cheating, I was furious, of course, but I got over it. I'm not the type to sit around and suffer all the time."

135

Perhaps the burden wasn't Dad so much as her own pride. Yes, I remember. When I was in my teens she treated me more as a friend and confidante than a daughter. Sometimes, as we strolled in the corridor, a small incident, a peripheral memory, would set her off, start her telling her Rosary of resentments.

"Nicaragua? Never!" she bursts out after Dad leaves for the Casino. "Imagine, Carmen! We arrived there just after our honeymoon, and the first thing Margarita told me after we'd met was: 'Oh, we're all so-o-o glad you married Alfonso. We were afraid he was going to marry that little tramp in Acajutla who gave him a son...Oh, my goodness!' she pretended to be so shocked, 'You mean he hasn't told you about that?'"

Mother interlaces her fingers, twists her hands, peers at me, demanding sympathy.

"Ah, if that had been the only time, Carmen, I might have forgotten. But it wasn't. It's happened time and again..."

I listened to her, a hard, uncomfortable knot of anger choking me: anger and resentment against Dad, and anger at her for burdening me with her complaints.

She suspected him of carrying on with some of his women patients. Occasionally at night, lying in bed, I would hear them quarreling in the patio, Dad fending off her accusations with a laugh and a denial. That wasn't like Dad, either. It would have been more in keeping with his character to match her anger with his own, to silence her with a peremptory bellow. But he never lost his patience at those times. Perhaps he wasn't as insensitive as Frank believed him to be. Maybe he had an intuition that if he reacted in any other way he might be opening a Pandora's box with unimaginable consequences for his life and all of ours.

No, Mother was out of character when she gave way to her suspicions and resentments, and Dad also in his way of turning them aside.

"She was worried about you these last months," Eugenia continues. "She said your letters sounded as though you were unhappy in Washington. And she was so anxious to see James and Lisa again."

"We were planning to come this next Christmas. Everything happened so quickly."

Silence enfolds us and our thoughts of her: a nostalgic quiet, underlined by crickets chirping under the flagstones, the subdued buzz of voices from the wake across the street.

"What did she do in the last months?"

"She followed the same routine as usual. She spent as much time reading as I do playing canasta," Eugenia smiles. "And she was more religious than ever; she never missed Mass in the mornings."

"Were she and Dad any closer?"

"I don't know, Carmen. They loved each other, no doubt of that. They'd lived together forty years. But they were so different from each other that they never talked a great deal. I think this house was silent most of the time, except when there were visitors. Alfredo entertained her. He would come by each noon with one or another of the children, or he and Ana would drop over in the evening. He made Isabel laugh at his jokes and his clowning. Whenever he didn't turn up she would start worrying, because she knew he was drinking again."

"How was Mother towards the last?" I asked Alfredo a few days ago.

"The same as always," he answered. "I miss her a lot, Carmen. It's hard to get used to her not being around any more with her advice and encouragement. She was always the lightning rod, you know, whenever Dad started thundering at me. The children loved her; she would read them stories or passages from the Bible. It was only in the last three months

137

that she started losing her strength and staying in bed longer that usual in the mornings."

"What was Frank like, Eugenia? Is there a photograph of him anywhere?"

"Not that I know of. I scarcely knew him, but I was the last one to see him. A few days after the uprising he came to the house. I told him I had delivered the letter he had written Isabel from San Salvador. 'Thank you,' he said, 'but it's too late for that. Please give her this package and tell her goodbye for me.'"

"Did you read the diary?"

"No. I've had it in my hands twice now, but I never opened it. It was wrapped when Isabel asked me to pass it to you. It was the day they took her to the hospital."

"Why do you think she left it for me?"

"I don't know, Carmen."

"This way, *hija.* Come with me." Dad, ten years older, a hundred years; no, a child, sobbing like a child, shuffles beside me toward the salon, his arm around my shoulders, but I'm supporting him. Avid eyes follow our progress. People crowd around me. People everywhere in the corridors, jamming the patio. Thank you, I say. Yes, thank you.

"Shall we go see her?"

"No, not yet." I don't want to see her yet. The bedroom, and I close the door or they'll follow us in here to sniff hungrily at our sorrow. I sit down at her vanity, wipe his tears from my cheek, run her silver brush through my hair, eye my stiff, unresponsive face in the mirror and wonder when my own tears will come.

"She was thinking of you when she went under the anaesthetic. 'Prepare Carmen for the news,' she told me. 'It's so much harder when one is far away.' And the

138

operation...useless. She's gone, Carmen. I don't want to go on living without her."

"Did she leave any of her diaries, Eugenia? She always kept a diary, but I've looked everywhere."
"She must have burned them."
"Didn't she even leave me a letter?"
"Nothing."
"Do you think Dad ever suspected about Frank?"
"I don't think so, but who knows? All of us would rather deceive ouselves than face something too painful to bear."

"How do you remember her?" I asked him yesterday.
"You knew her," he answers slowly, his rocking chair scarcely moving. "There's no reason for anything now that she's gone. I ask myself now if I made her happy. I tried, in my way, but we were very different, your mother and I. Sometimes I couldn't understand her; sometimes I hurt her without meaning to. But a whole lifetime together, Carmen," he peers at me pensively, "has to be more than just happiness. It has to be more than an accident."

"I'm sleepy," Eugenia rises and stretches. "Aren't you coming to bed yet?"
"No. It's cool here. And I want to finish the diary."
I accompany her to the bedroom, return with Frank's notebook, and settle down under the lamp in the corridor. The wake across the street has run its course, and all of Santa Ana is asleep.
This is what she had; nothing more than this: Santa Ana and its unchanging faces, its small tragedies and comedies and scandals; Dad with his bluff manner and his acceptance of the world he could see and touch; Alfredo, myself, the rest of the family, and — for a brief instant — Frank. A tiny, self-

139

enclosed, monotint world which laid bare the illusion of time and seeming change.

Frank, I think, altered the course of her life. I really don't know. Had she lived in Paris, for example, and had it all happened there, perhaps she might have solved the problem. But Frank here in Santa Ana proved to be an obstacle she was never able to surmount or bypass or demolish. Had he never appeared, Mother might have been able to accept this small world and its conventions, Dad's occasional infidelities, her own assigned role as mother and doctor's wife; but he — the outsider — opened the door on another possible world. Which of them finally closed that door: he or she?

However it was, she could never forget that one glimpse, could never afterwards mold herself to the demands of Santa Ana, and so she became in turn Dad's obstacle: the Chinese puzzle he never could solve.

There are other doors in the world than the Washington door, the Paul door. I could open them; I could take the children to Mexico and find a job there. I've thought about it many times, have run around inside the thought like a squirrel in a treadmill until I'm worn out. There has been the poetess door, the actress door, and I passed them by. There's a purple door ajar as I sleepwalk through my house. Why does purple frighten us? I have talent, I tell myself. I could write or paint or act if I worked at any of those things, but I sleepwalk. For a man it's different, I tell myself. It's easier for a man to push new doors open. That's not true. If I had really felt an urge, I could have pursued it. I've tried writing, but I have nothing to say that would interest anybody else. What comes out on the page is self-pity. Self-pity for what? Because I'm empty inside? Is it a long, thin whine at the injustice of Carmen not being what Carmen always imagined herself to be? I look down on Paul because he lacks passion, but what have I ever hurled myself into blindly, confidently? Am I afraid of losing my central heating, my car, my television set? Am I merely afraid to be alone with my emptiness?

I used to be different, thirsty for the world, for new faces, new cities, new experiences: a wide-eyed, coltish enthusiasm. Where has that feeling gone? All the faces are the same now; I don't look at streets or buildings; my own face in the mirror is blank as I color its lips, pencil its eyebrows: an oval, expressionless face, with emptiness singing inside it like a wail of muted pain. Paul is empty too, and he hides it in his way. He needs me, but I can't help him. I have nothing to give, nothing to say that hasn't been emptied of meaning by repetition. James and Lisa need me, but one day soon they'll notice they have a hollow mother. I think about myself too much, and they say that's bad. Maybe that's the trouble: a circular thought orbiting around a zero. Think, instead, about Mother, sitting here day after day with her thoughts, her memories, her preoccupations.

Her face is slipping away from me already, dissolving into emptiness. Which face of Mother? The last one. Only the last one in the candlelight, smoothed and emptied and as still as the cold hands with the Rosary twined about them.

They placed Mama Carmen's bones, wrapped in a sheet, at her feet. Dad sobbed aloud as he closed the lid over her. Alfredo, Rodolfo, Augusto and Eduardo lifted the coffin and jostled through the door carrying it shoulder-high. Eight blocks under the afternoon sun, they carried it, Ana and I behind on either side of Dad, and the stream of others behind us, with only the sound of feet rasping over the cobblestones.

The hearse waited at the edge of town. The procession dissolved into a mob of people wiping their foreheads with handkerchiefs and fanning themselves. We followed the hearse slowly past the *ceiba*, and the ladies who sell *pupusas* crossed themselves and kissed their thumbs solemnly. We crept past Don Jaime's coffee mill, past the small, green river where the washerwomen, stripped naked to the waist, looked up and fell silent. The *maquilishuats* were in bloom. We passed another funeral procession, a child's, with a white coffin and gaily-colored ribbons. We reached the cemetery.

Dad stumbled getting out of the car, but Alfredo caught and supported him. We walked behind the coffin to the family plot where Mama Carmen's grave lay open, waiting. Father Antonio, ageless, indestructible, recited interminable prayers. Dad held an arm about my shoulders; his tremblings communicating themselves to me. He was weeping, but I couldn't, not even when they lowered the coffin, slung between wide bands, into the gaping hole.

Chapter Sixteen

Isabel:

I hear the echo of your voice repeating your last words to me, and I must think carefully, Isabel; it is so important for you and for me.

I know how difficult these last days have been for you as you hunted back and forth along the same path of thought time and again. But you must understand: that last phrase was not spoken by you; it was dictated by pressures and conventions that have been bearing down on you ever since childhood and that have blinded you now. If you surrender to them, allow yourself to remain their captive, you will be lost, Isabel, and so will I.

You're made from a different mold than Santa Ana's. Your vitality, your thirst for a richer, fuller life, will turn against you if you choose to remain here. Have you glimpsed the interminable file of gray days and months and years stretching out ahead, waiting to be filled with your self-abnegation, remorse, and the haunting thought that life might have been otherwise?

I recognized your need when I first saw you, my darling, and I determined to snatch you from the edge of the *cenote*, to ride away with you toward a more generous future: one with variegated landscapes, new faces, new sounds. I thought also, as you have so many times, of Carmen and Alfredo and of their future. I wanted to help give them a chance to lead fuller lives than they can ever find here.

And I thought of my own need, Isabel. You cannot be a lifesaver tossed to me and then, as my fingers close on it, snatched away. You cannot be a mere event, an episode, in my life; nor an accident, a cruel joke. I am a dark planet which has found for the first time its exact orbit around a light-giving sun. You dare not condemn me to wander again through the dark night and the cold wind of space.

Isabel:

Your last words keep echoing in my head:

"We can never see each other again. We can never see each other again. We can never..."

Each time I have answered them, repeating:

"No. This cannot end so stupidly."

But at the thousandth repetition I betrayed myself, caught myself wondering:

"Can this really end so stupidly?"

The very grounds of sanity slipped away, merely because I had posed the question. I am sliding, falling, Isabel. My mind tears frantically in circles, leaps at the walls, falls back. I can't write, Isabel; I write in circles too. Now that you have forbidden me your face, your voice — now that it is more necessary than ever before to wield a convincing, authoritative pen, one that moves unhesitatingly, irresistibly — I find that I have been drained of thought; I am empty.

Emptiness, terror, the need to summon strength somehow, have brought me here to the bar of the Hotel Florida. I haven't missed alcohol for some time. I sip it now slowly, without desire, as one takes a medical prescription, in order to be able to write you the things I must say. It's beginning to bring results as it always did before. The pounding pulse in my temples diminishes. Your voice keeps repeating the same refrain, but it's more distant now: it comes to me from far away, from another room, another world, that I am leaving behind. My mind was feverish, overheated, but that is all changing as the medicine trickles into my veins.

That's the boy, Frank! A few more sips now and you'll feel it, cool, cooler, ice cold. That's it. As cold and transparent as a cube of ice floating in a highball. The old, frozen *Satori*, the authentic article, knocking, tugging, prying at the brain.

Take another sip. And another.

Now he takes a little one.

Now.

144

And he rose once more, suspended by the silver cord, nearly to the ceiling. He looked down at himself seated in the chair, the fourth whisky within comfortable reach, absorbed in his scribbling. He noticed that his neck had been reddened by the Santa Ana sun and that the barber yesterday had left him with a fringe of white skin at the hairline behind the ears. It felt great to be floating free again. He smiled happily, and the rag doll below echoed him, smiled stupidly into its notebook. Once again, in a flash, he saw with great, transparent, ice cube clarity, the absurd *why* of everything, he grasped in its entirety the meaningless pattern he had been weaving across the woof of days and years on the cosmic loom. It was so ridiculous he laughed aloud. The noise startled him, and he felt himself dropping like a punctured balloon. The figure at the table hastily raised the glass to its lips. Once more, as the liquid cut an icy path down his throat, he stabilized and tugged gently upward to the ceiling.

"Poor old Frank!" he thought. "Poor old stupid Frank. He's never been able to understand these things, but I'm going to help him. We'll make a crackerjack team, the two of us. We'll start now by setting a few blunt truths down on paper."

The powerful winch in his brain rolled up the cord, and again he was seated at the table, staring down at the notebook.

Isabel (he began to write rapidly, surely) is a product of her environment. It is not merely that Santa Ana is a small, underdeveloped corner of Hell, but even more important is the fact that its settlers brought to it the seeds of immemorial fears and prejudices — the kind that seem to be transmitted through the blood, absorbed along with mother's milk.

Individuals spring up here; there's no doubt about that. Take Alfonso, for example: like all Spaniards, he is a ferocious individualist. The people I have met here bear their eccentricities, like the mark of Cain, blazoned on their foreheads. Alongside this, perhaps because of it, there is a tremendous rigidity of form, a decorum and punctiliousness akin to the Bushido. From the cradle onward, the individual

145

is free in one dimension of ego to flourish as voraciously and raggedly as a blackberry vine, but his windward, social side is clipped and pruned and trimmed back by a patriarchal, family tyrant who is abetted by a submissive, fear-stricken mother; by a Church which wields the shears of brimstone and damnation, by a host of gossiping, prying, convention-ridden, class-conscious aunts, uncles, grandparents, teachers, priests, and other casual, self-appointed guardians of small-town morality.

You, Isabel, have been unable to push past these miserable barriers. You are alive, imaginative, curious, and you know that Santa Ana's mold will deform you; you know you must break out and leave behind these people who cannot understand you, who will come — over the years — to look at you as just one more eccentric with your potted begonias and French novels. You have bowed down to them, Isabel. You have fallen on your knees to pacify the absurd fears of your childhood, the nonexistent ghosts your imagination has been taught to project.

They are all unreal, but our love is real. It exists. The two of us have touched it, lived it. You know as certainly as I do that we cannot live without each other.

Think about it, Isabel. I will give you the time you need to weigh our love against the sterility that surrounds you here. You know another world exists; your books have told you that much. I have seen that world and lived in it, but without you, whom I need.

The trouble is that you lack daring, you have not yet nerved yourself up to make the leap. The problem is: you were born a woman in Santa Ana. But all you have to do is leave it. The answer is so simple. Can't you see it, my darling?

He closed the notebook, sipped the last of his drink, and went to the bar to pay his check. He bought a bottle to take with him. Fine! Notebook in pocket, bottle under arm, and off we go under the hot sun.

146

"You're going to burn your neck," he told himself, and then, softly: "Isabel, you are a coward."

He walked with springy step, smiled benevolently at two little girls playing hopscotch on the sidewalk. He whistled a series of crystalline, separate notes, and with each note he imagined himself landing on one springy leg in another square.

"You don't love Alfonso," he told her. "He has deceived you. Besides, he treats you like a wife, like private property, like a piece of goods."

He smiled wolfishly.

"You are a good little piece, Isabel."

An old woman, laden with bundles, glanced at him, startled.

He crossed cobbled streets, cut through Santa Lucia park and flipped a salute at the stone virgin, entered the house, uncorked the bottle, poured a half-glass, added a smidgin of water, sank down in Virgil's chair, raised the glass to eye level, and looked at the amber liquid.

"So we can't see each other again," he said.

He drank the whisky thoughtfully. He pulled out his notebook and scribbled for some minutes between the remaining sips. The house was hot beneath the afternoon sun. He decided to take a little nap.

January 18, 1932

Make following points:

A. Have not written or tried see you past five days to give you time reconsider, to weigh richness of our love against sterility Sta. Ana. You must have spent these days pondering gray emptiness ahead, etc...

B. I know it more than bonds of convention that holds you here, but I also know you too liberated, mature, to let absurd small-town mores dictate your life. Ties of love and affection for your family also bind you, emotional threads linking you to father, brothers and sisters. But you must not let them conduct your life for you.

147

C. Know you also have doubts about what best for Carmen and Alfredo. But you already know what is best. I offer them and you wider horizons, opportunities, the whole outside world. (Careful how you phrase this.)

D. The argument that you have an obligation to Alfonso, that he's the father of your children, is not convincing. He is an admirable individual, but has never made you happy, never understood you as I understand you. He's self-centered, self-sufficient. To him you're a wife, mother, housekeeper, much as a flower pot is a flower pot. His medicine, billiards, chess, Central American unity, fill his life. If one flower pot disappears, he will simply find another and carry on without breaking stride.

E. New reservations for 29th. Returning Sta. Ana early 23rd. Must see you. Time growing short now.

F. I love you, etc. Don't remain a flower pot the rest of your days, Isabel. I ask you instead to be my companion, partner, lover, fellow-adventurer, mistress, wife.

(Have Eugenia deliver it personally. Should get there on 20th.)

Chapter Seventeen

January 27, 1932

Isabel:

Eugenia will give you this after I'm gone. When you have finished reading it, throw it away or burn it.

Where to start? First, I have been drinking or drunk more or less constantly since I last saw you two weeks ago. I have been in San Salvador to cancel the passages I had requested and to make new reservations, and I caught the late bus back on the night of the 22nd to reach you the following morning as I had promised in my letter. I took a seat in the back and concentrated on not taking a nip from the hip flask I carried. I didn't want to be hung over or still drunk when I talked to you.

We were near Coatepeque when the driver slammed on the brakes, and suddenly the bus was surrounded by a crowd of men armed with *machetes*. The driver resisted when they dragged him out, and one of them cut him down with a slice that nearly severed his head. They looted each passenger as he stepped out the door and bundled each one off into the grove beside the road. There was a pretty, young girl several seats ahead of me, and one of the peasants who had entered the bus pulled her out and dragged her off, screaming and scratching, in a different direction. I managed to stuff a few bills and my passport under my belt, and I handed over my suitcase and my wallet as I got off. I told the man who took them that I was an American and a tourist. It didn't impress him.

"This bus can be useful to carry your men," I suggested. "I can drive it for you."

He thought about it, eyeing me suspiciously. Another car stopped behind us, and the driver tried frantically to make a U-turn in the narrow road. He was unsuccessful, and the new arrivals were hauled out by the mob. That distraction seemed to swing the balance in my favor. The leader singled out an unshaven brute to accompany me, and told me to park the bus a short way up the road. The guard sat behind me with his *machete* lying across his lap. As I pulled the bus out of the confusion I could see a cluster of figures silhouetted against oncoming headlights several hundred yards up the road. Another group there was stopping cars coming from Santa Ana.

I remained in the driver's seat, trembling spasmodically from the reaction, for perhaps fifteen or twenty minutes. At the end of that time a group of about two dozen men crammed into the bus, and I started the motor.

"Take us to *La Milagrosa*," their leader ordered me.

"I don't know the place," I told him. "You'll have to guide me."

We turned off the main highway to the left, and I steered down a narrow, dirt road, our headlights picking out the gray ghosts of coffee trees on either side of us. The men behind me were excited, laughing and shouting to each other loudly over the roar of the motor. I didn't recognize the road until the lake came in sight, silvery flat in the moonlight. We headed down, drove along the edge, and toiled upward over the stretch of road where Alfonso and I had gotten stuck; up, interminably, past the cemetery where we had let the funeral party off and had then turned back. I wondered if either of the two men who had ridden with us that day was in the bus behind me now. Ahead of us to the right, a heavy black cloud illuminated by an intermittent orange glow marked the location of Izalco.

After perhaps half an hour of steady, slow climbing up the inner rim of the crater, the road curved downward again. It straightened into a steep dip, and we picked up speed. I shifted unobtrusively into neutral, pushed the driver's door open, and flung myself out. I landed with a jarring wrench and managed one or two crazy, sprawling steps alongside the bus before I hurtled into the embankment with a crash that nearly knocked me out. I lay there sobbing with the pain of my wrenched hip, still unaware of the deep gashes in my palms and forearms where I had broken my fall. I raised my head to look down the road where the bus was veering crazily from side to side as someone tried to take control of the wheel. It grazed the right embankment at an angle, reared upward, teetered, and fell over on its side.

I pulled myself up the bank and started limping, hobbling, uphill through the coffee trees as rapidly as I could. Each step was agonizing pain. I paused every few yards out of sheer inability to go on, and I listened for sounds of pursuit. The moon was sinking now, dim and red in the haze of high ashes thrown up by the volcano.

I remembered the hip flask. Miraculously, it was intact, and I swallowed a helpful gulp of whisky. It took me several hours to reach the rim of the crater, although I probably covered no more than two kilometers. On the other side I gave out completely, crawled into one of the brush-covered gullies, and lay resting in a coffin-sized space beneath a bush. Another swallow of whisky helped me into a fitful, pain-shot sleep, complicated by mosquitos and the night chill.

I awoke at dawn and found that my hip would not support my weight. I was crazed with thirst and dragged myself down the gully until I found a pool of stagnant water. I tried to think about my situation, but I had few facts to go on. The mob at Coatepeque had been much too large to be a gang of bandits, so I assumed they must have been part of an organized uprising. I had no way of knowing how widespread the movement might be. I was certain, however, that things were bad in the area that lay between me and Santa Ana, and I decided that I should head in the opposite direction. I also calculated that anyone I met in these surroundings would be more likely to cut my throat than to help me.

It took an entire morning of Indian scout crawling to find a forked branch that could serve as a crutch and to gnaw it to the right length with a sharp rock. I drank more water and slept a little during the afternoon, unmolested by cold and mosquitos, less sensitive to the throbbing of my hip.

151

In the evening I crawled up to the rim of the crater again, alert to any signs of movement, and when night fell I started hobbling slowly in the direcon of the smoke cloud that marked Izalco.

It took some time to learn how to handle the crutch, but after the first half hour my hip limbered up a bit, and I was able to put some weight on it. I was growing hungry in spite of the pain, but no matter.

It was a weird, unforgettable night. Izalco was in constant eruption, and the breeze brought me its intermittent growl and a shower of fine, gray ashes that sifted down, covering the ground, the trees, my clothing, and occasionally getting into my eyes with a sulphurous bite. The dark cloud of smoke rolled uninterruptedly overhead, blacking out the moon and the stars. The only landmark was the red flow from the volcano. Other than that, the world was a jumble of dim trees, shrubs, treacherous pitfalls and painful toil.

A childhood remembrance flickered in the back of my mind, something allied with the pedal organ in the parlor, suggestive of the thick book of illustrated Bible stories that provided my first literary excursions. Finally I placed it: *Pilgrim's Progress*, of course! I, Frank Christian Goodfellow, continued limping beneath the cloud of ashes along my hillside of pain, cursing Bunyan's overactive imagination. I thought about you, Isabel, and put the thought out of my mind, because there was nothing to be done about you until I got through the present ordeal.

The flask of whisky gurgled in my pocket each time my crutch struck down, and I thought about that for a while. I had no desire for a drink. I had make up my mind to hoard what was left in the bottle as an energy surrogate which I would surely need before this absurd trial came to an end. But it was there, gurgling with every step, and I was carrying its small weight as well as my own. What with pain, hunger, near-delirium, and ashes drifting down in my face while the pulsating fulguration ahead lit up the trees and the way ever more strongly, I saw clearly for a moment that I, Frank

Christian Barleycorn, was nothing more than a skin enwrapping a shadow that detested it, that was determined to stun, desensitize and drown that shabby garment in fiery, sloshing liquid. I stumped along, carrying the bottle and my unknown, unknowable host.

Next, it occured to me that I had tricked myself once again: that I had set up my quest of Isabel knowing it to be hopeless; that I had set the whole plot in motion to provide myself with a valid emotional excuse to go back to the bottle when you turned me down. My nerve endings had outsmarted me once more; I was a rag doll being manipulated by an atavistic, ravening thirst.

It was at this point that I nearly threw the bottle away. I determined that I would override my internal clamorings, I would not let you or anyone ever catch me off guard again. I made up my mind that I would go back on the wagon, nevermore to touch a drop. I had proved I could do it for three long months, and toward the last I hardly ever missed it. Had I not lost my footing accidentally, I would still be holding out. I'd learned to endure that sensation. I might even learn to live with it and to do something useful and productive in spite of it, or even because of it. I stopped and reached into my pocket to pull the flask out and hurl it from me when it occurred to me that the flask was the only container I had in case I found water somewhere, and a man can go without food for days, but he'll go mad without water. I left it there and started hobbling forward into the center of hell once more.

I thought aimlessly about the sanitorium and how comfortable the white bed, the white-uniformed nurses, and kindly, patriarchal, good old Doc Adams, had been. I thought about my imginary squirrels and birds and rabbits wintering in the cool white snow around my Sierra lake, and how wonderful it would be to drowse in the cabin with a fire going rather than limping along as I was through a crazed and hostile world.

Gradually, I stopped feeling sorry for myself as I fumbled for another thought that lay in the red, tree-silhouetting

153

glow ahead of me. This wasn't, I understood, a run of bad luck, a series of disagreeeable experiences, a punishment dealt out to me for my loose behavior. It was, instead, a *Via Crucis*, an education, a maze that I, Frank Christian Barleycorn Laboratory Rat I, was being taught with electrical prods on the behind goading me forward into the impossible, the unthinkable.

You cannot escape what you are. (I must have said the words out loud.) You don't have to like what you are, but you cannot run away from the fact of yourself, nor can you push yourself off on other people and beg them to take responsibility for you. No more can Isabel escape herself, I thought, escape being a tropical flower, a rare and beautiful orchid that I saw and prized and wished to pluck.

I was close to Izalco by now. The thick pillar of greasy smoke boiled upward above the trees; the cloud overhead was no longer diffused, but was a tangible ceiling — the roof of a demon-haunted cavern — racing away toward the lake, pulsating with a pink blush at every new eruption. The rumble of each explosion was as deafening now as the sound of a fast express crossing a trestle, but one can become accustomed to anything, even to such incredible sensory assaults as I was undergoing. I picked my way along a path illuminated by the reflected light from above.

The ground and trees fell away to my left. I rounded a bend and stopped dead still in shock. The cone of Izalco itself rose before me in all its fury and splendor. There, in the middle of the night, no more than two kilometers away, it reared its fiery head almost to eye level. The crater was an angry wound limned in incandescent lava. As I watched, a new explosion tore the gaping mouth open and threw a fountain of lava hundreds of feet in the air. The sheet of liquid rock rose, divided into fiery sparks that arced outward through the belch of black smoke squirting horizontally from the sides of the crater. Fragments the size of automobiles, of houses, crashed against the sides of the cone and bounded down the steep slope in an orange blaze. A tide from the lava lake pushed through a fissure in the side of the crater nearest me and started spilling in slow motion down the sloping wall, pulsing and sparkling with an eery mineral life. A pathway of lava, mottled with black and glowing red, reached from the fissure all the way down the side of the cone and widened into a smoking, orange-colored delta at the base. As I stood paralyzed, the stream suddenly became Tlaloc's mighty arm reaching out to bury its spreading fingers in his soil. He was awake and about to push himself erect out of the crater to stalk his land once more, sowing terror and death and destruction.

I limped forward slowly, my eyes fixed on the cone and the thick, writhing fan billowing from it. At one point my crutch sank in the mud, and I discovered a rivulet of water trickling downhill across my path. I followed it upstream a few yards and drank. The water had a sulphurous taste from the volcanic ash dissolved in it, but I was thirsty. I decided to fill my flask and held it up against the light from the cone to discover it was still half full.

No, I didn't pour out the whisky. I told myself I needed the energy it would give me. I knelt down and let a trickle of water fill it. Then I took my sulphur highball down the slope a way, sat with my back against a rock, and started drinking, while Chac raged and bellowed at me and struggled to clamber out through his chimney to crush me in his red fist.

I raised my flask in salute.

"My last drink," I assured him solemnly, and I let it run down my throat. The water cut the whisky, and the whisky burned away the sulphurous flavor of the water. On the whole, it wasn't a bad combination, and I had a full flask to work on: enough, at my present low level of resistance, to get me beautifully besodden. After the first gulp I sipped at it slowly, never taking my eyes from the volcano.

"If you were only a camera, Frank," I thought, "if you could only capture this scene just as it is, you would be doing something worthwhile. If you were only a lousy movie camera, you could do it."

155

I set the flask down carefully, made a frame with my two hands, and panned the scene slowly as another explosion hurled lava skyward and shook the ground under me.

"But you're not even a lousy camera, Frank. And even if you were, you undoubtedly would have run out of film before you ever got up here."

I sighed and went on with a previous, interrupted thought: She knew it without knowing the *why* of the words, and all she could say was,

"We can never see each other again."

That is her wisdom, and there's no quarreling with it. And probably in some inner reach of intuition she recognized that you had invented her, conjured up a mirage, a self-induced hallucination; that you had told yourself a milennial bedtime story and, in your desperation and self-serving malice, had come to believe in it even as you were planning and manipulating the next of the innumerable changes that can be rung on the theme of the travelling salesman and the farmer's daughter, the world-weary writer and the small-town doctor's wife, the unregenerate drunk and the immaterial wraith fleeing before him: a figment of his feverish imaginings that might save him from himself.

I stopped short and started thinking about the peasants in the bus that had crashed against the embankment. I hadn't thought of them until now.

"But I do love her; I do need her."

I finished the flask without lowering it from my lips. For an instant, beneath the sky, with Izalco raging and drooling incandescent lava like a colossal imbecile, I felt once again the approach to *Satori*. This time I said no.

"To hell with your *Satori*," I said, "and your *karma* and your *dharma*; with your idiotic reincarnation and your Boy Scout merit badges." If all that were true, Isabel, it would be horrible. What I want is a forgetting, a dark, interminable sleep.

Despite Izalco's roarings and shakings, I slept there. In the morning I filled my flask with water and set off again along the side of *Cerro Verde*, my stomach rubbing against my backbone. There were no berries, no bananas, nothing but brush, grass and a few spindly trees on the poisoned hillside. No people either.

The village of Izalco came in sight from behind the flank of the volcano, and I strained my eyes staring at it from five kilometers away. It seemed peaceful, somnolent. From that distance I could detect no evidences of abnormality, and I began to believe that my adventure of two nights before had been merely an isolated incident. It was the atmosphere of political tension since last month's coup that had gotten my wind up, I told myself; it had been all of Eduardo's talk about an impending night of long knives, which salted the Christmas Eve conversation of Santa Ana's rich folk that had made me think there was a revolt; and I spent two days hiding in the hills for no reason at all.

Putting the crater behind me, I threw aside caution and started quartering down the steep slope. My leg was better, and I used the crutch only as a staff to ease my descent. By mid-morning I was back in coffee country, striding confidently through the trees. Suddenly I found myself in a clearing. A small, thatched hut stood at one edge, and an Indian woman gazed at me curiously from the doorway. Several youngsters fled to refuge behind her skirts. I felt uneasy, but I sensed it would be a mistake to flee.

I walked boldly across the clearing and asked her if I could buy some food. Without a word, she ladled a gob of black beans onto a tortilla and handed it to me. My trepidation vanished under the onslaught of hunger. I wolfed down the tortilla and topped it off with two bananas and a drink of cold, nonsulphurous water from an earthenware jug. The woman gravely refused the coins I offered her, pointed out the direction of Izalco, and ordered one of the children to accompany me to the main road. I thanked her and set off behind my silent guide, feeling that I was well out of danger.

The boy disappeared into the trees as soon as I reached the edge of the road, and I started sauntering toward Izalco, feeling something akin to cheerfulness and well-being.

Minutes later I was stopped by an army patrol under the command of a civilian wearing a white arm band. The soldiers were advancing along the sides of the road in scouting formation, with their rifles at the ready and bayonets fixed. I told my story briefly to the patrol leader, without dwelling on the details of my escape from the bus. He shook his head and assured me I bore a charmed life.

"That same night," he told me, "peasant bands attacked half a dozen towns around here and occupied four of them, including Izalco. We took Izalco back yesterday in four hours of street fighting. Had to clean them out block by block. All the other towns have been recovered too."

My kaleidescope world twisted abruptly and fell back into the pattern I had visualized until a few hours before.

"Santa Ana?" I asked, remembering the Guard barrackes in front of your house. "Was it attacked?"

He shook his head.

"Some shooting outside the town, but nothing serious."

"What is Izalco like?"

"It's safe enough now," he told me. "We've disarmed everybody in the immediate area, and we're starting to work through the *fincas* now." His face twisted into a bitter mask. "They killed my brother and his whole family." He turned away abruptly and waved his patrol forward.

I walked through a strange hush toward Izalco. There was no movement along the road, such as I had become accustomed to, no workers grubbing among the coffee trees, no women or children outside the occasional huts I passed. Yet I felt I was being watched.

It finally happened, I thought: the explosion Eduardo had foretold — how long ago was it? — and the certain repression by uniformed troops that Don Manuel had predicted as an aftermath. I wondered where Martí, the man who had tried to saddle the cyclone, was now. His *finca,* which I had visited a few weeks before, could not be more than a few miles from where I found myself. And I had spent the two days of the brief, bloody civil war sleeping in ravines and on hillsides, limping through the sulphurous wilderness, unaware of it all. The sky was clear overhead, but behind me the eery, inky cloud from Izalco boiled away toward Santa Ana.

"Isabel will be watching it," I told myself, "looking at the dark, sunless sky and the ashes raining down, and thinking about the fighting and killing of these last days."

I wondered if you had been thinking of me. I stopped the thought and walked on.

There were soldiers on guard at every street corner in Izalco and a company of reserve troops in the central plaza. Bullets had dug brown wounds in the whitewashed adobe walls. Here and there along the street were dark patches of dried blood. Except for the soldiers, I sensed the same hush, the same suspension of normal activity, that I'd noticed in the countryside.

A military command post had been set up in the mayor's office across the square from the church with its white facade and single bell tower. I presented my passport to one of the sentries, and within a few minutes I was ushered into the office where an army captain sat behind the lone desk.

I told him my story, again skipping the details. He accepted it, nodding as I spoke.

"I must get to Santa Ana immediately," I told him. "How can I do it?"

He shrugged.

"All trucks and buses have been commandeered for use by the army," he said. "As of now, there is no public transport. I'm afraid there's nothing I can do to help you."

I asked if I could catch a ride to Santa Ana on any vehicle that might be returning there. He shook his head firmly.

"Sorry. Army and Civil Guard personnel only. I can't disobey my orders."

159

"Can I rent a private automobile, a horse, anything?" I persisted. He shook his head impatiently.

"We're using everything in town. This is a military zone of operations, *Señor*, and it would be extremely dangerous for you to leave Izalco until order is restored."

He handed back my passport, putting an end to the interview. I limped out into the sun with no idea of what to do next. Walking any further was unthinkable. I was still hungry, so I made my way to the *cantina* at one side of the main square and ordered a large meal. The owner, a wizened little old lady, had one of the few telephones in town, and after lunch I put through a call to Eduardo in Santa Ana. I ordered another beer while waiting for the connection and struck up a conversation with the old lady.

"What happened here?" I asked her.

Her wrinkles rearranged themselves in an expression of anguish.

"Ah, I tell you it was terrible!" she wailed. "They slipped down from the hills at night with their *machetes*. I woke up with the shooting around the National Guard post, and suddenly the town was full of them, shouting and banging on doors looking for weapons. They made me open the *cantina*, and then they sat around here, waiting."

"In the morning," she continued, "they dragged Don Indalecio, the mayor, and Don Benjamin and half a dozen others out into the plaza and chopped them to bits." She rubbed the back of one hand distractedly. "Chopped them to bits and left them lying there," she repeated.

"The soldiers came yesterday afternoon. Everybody rushed around when the shooting started, but I didn't see what happened. I put the bottles on the floor and hid behind the barrels until it was all over. It was terrible! Terrible!"

When I got Eduardo on the line I had trouble convincing him I had walked through the bloodiest region in the country during the preceding two days.

160

"Monstrous things have been happening, Frank," his voice trembled. "And now the army and Civil Guard are hunting peasants in packs, shooting them like animals."

I remembered the arc of the *machete* swinging down on the bus driver's head, the screams of the girl who was dragged away into the darkness.

"Our generation is stained with blood," his words came to me sepulchrally through the receiver. "There can be no forgiveness for such crimes."

"Was it Martí who set the peasants off?" I asked.

"Martí was arrested in San Salvador three days before the uprising. Hadn't you heard?"

I confessed I hadn't been reading the papers.

I don't know, Frank. I don't believe he was responsible; he was trying to hold them back and play for time. I think everything fell apart when he was arrested."

He asked me about the situation in Izalco, and I told him what little I knew. Then I explained that I was stranded and asked if he could come and pick me up in his car.

"I wish I could, but I can't get away. We're so overworked that I've been living in the newspaper office, catching naps on the floor now and then, ever since this started."

He promised, though, that he would send somebody else with his car to fetch me. I thanked him and told him I would be waiting in the *cantina*.

I went outside and wandered about on the off chance that I might be able to hail a ride in a car leaving this dead village. But, except for the soldiers, there was no movement. The people of Izalco were sitting behind their closed doors, their shuttered windows, waiting.

It was late afternoon now, and I returned to the *cantina*. There were a few off-duty soldiers standing at the bar and seated at one of the tables. They were subdued; the hush of Izalco had communicated itself to them, and they stared down at their glasses or exchanged occasional low comments with each other. After the first appraisal they ignored me, and I them.

161

I sat at my corner table, and the old lady brought me beer. It's strange: being an alcoholic, whisky or any other strong drink goes to my head immediately. Beer, on the other hand, doesn't affect me noticeably, and I can go on drinking day and night.

I thought of us, Isabel, and I thought of myself with tenderness and pity.

I thought of Alfonso with impotent scorn: so admirable, such a sterling character, so sure of himself, so completely insensitive. He doesn't need you as I need you. I'll return, and Isabel will see me in my dirty, bloodstained clothing. I'll limp into the patio with a three-day-growth of beard. She will guess what horrors I have gone through to find my way back to her; she will realize how great is my need; she will soften, relent, change her mind, when she sees me that way.

I had absently marked each point with a coin laid down on the table before me, each in the exact center of a wet ring left by my glass. I stared at the geometric pattern, the interlacing rings of Frank Wolff's mind and personality and motives. The intercommunicating circles closed on themselves and led...where? I scooped up the coins, strode to the bar, and ordered a double *guaro*. After that I bought a whole bottle for myself, and gradually it grew later.

Nobody was coming to my rescue. The old lady confirmed my suspicion that there were no hotels in Izalco, but she offered to let me sleep on a pile of straw in the storeroom behind the *cantina*. I accepted, sight unseen, carried my bottle with me for warmth and company, and crawled into the dark little grotto she indicated.

She was a good old soul. The next morning she brought me a pan of water, soap and a towel, and she laughed merrily at my visible, creaking hangover. She prepared a breakfast of tortillas, beans, and strong coffee, and I slowly revived.

I walked over to the command post for another unsatisfactory interview with the captain, who didn't know and didn't care when the bus service would be resumed, and who was not going to be budged from his standing orders.

In contrast to the previous day, the plaza of Izalco was filling with peasants. Squads of soldiers guarded the street mouths leading into the main square, but I felt uneasy to see so many Indians in their straw hats and white, baggy trousers leaning against the walls, squatting in small groups on the cobblestones. None of them were carrying *machetes*, though, and the soldiers seemed to pay no attention to them.

I strolled toward the edge of town against the thickening tide of white blouses and pants that streamed in along the road by which I had entered the day before. Two army trucks were parked there, with lengthening queues of incoming peasants — all men — stretching down the road behind them.

Each of them, I saw, was surrendering his *machete* to the soldiers, and was receiving a white slip of paper in return.

"What's happening?" I asked the lieutenant who was supervising the operation.

"We're disarming all the people in this area," he replied. "Our patrols have spread the word that anyone caught with a *machete*, or anyone who cannot produce one of these safe-conduct passes," he gestured toward the two sergeants who were handing out the white slips, "will be shot after tomorrow."

Other soldiers were directing the disarmed Indians along the street toward the plaza.

"Why that?" I asked. The lieutenant shrugged.

"We've received word that General Calderón will be arriving this afternoon to address the people, and he wants them all assembled in the main plaza."

I walked back pensively. The measures being taken seemed stern, but they probably were justified under the circumstances. With a crowd of this size in town it would be difficult to locate me unless I remained faithfully in the *cantina*. I quickened my steps.

The old lady was doing a humming business today, but my corner table was still unoccupied. I settled down with a new bottle of *aguardiente* and the intention of working on it with the measured pace of a long-distance runner. There were no

163

soldiers among the clientele, only Indians down from the hills. The low buzz of their conversation had halted abruptly when I entered, and long, suspicious stares from the surrounding tables emphasized my feeling of being an unwelcome intruder. Should I smile? Bow? A gnarled, dark face at the next table gazed at me impassively over an empty glass. I grinned falsely, foolishly, and gestured invitingly toward my bottle. The man shook his head stolidly and looked away.

I drank carefully, keeping my eyes on the table, and gradually they lost their interest in me.

Gingerly, unwillingly, as a man removing the bandage over a gangrenous wound and dreading what it may reveal, I forced myself to think back beyond your last words:

"We can never see each other again, Frank."

What was it you said before that? What was the argument I had been trying to batter aside ever since?

"I've thought about us," you told me. "I've thought about nothing else these last days." We were seated at the table in Virgil's house, and you put your hand over mine.

"I don't regret what happened; it chose us. I love you, Frank. I hope you remember that always. I will."

And then, how did you phrase it?

"You are alone and need think only of your loneliness and your love, but I cannot obey my own selfishness; I must think of the three other lives that are bound to mine."

"The children are small," I protested. "They will forget Alfonso in a few months."

"He is their father," you said quietly. "They are his as well as mine, and he loves them." You looked at our hands interlaced on the table. "It would be different if he weren't a good man, the best father he knows how to be.

"Do I love him? Yes, in a different way than I love you. He offers strength, protection, a refuge against my own insecurity. I don't know."

You gripped my hands tightly, looked directly at me.

"You and I are too much alike, Frank. I've asked myself: is it just fear of the unknown? Am I merely clinging to my house, my servants, the security that Alfonso offers? Could I face a new world at your side, knowing that both of us share the same doubts and indecisions? I couldn't answer the question. Perhaps I am a coward."

I stared back mutely, unable to speak.

"But if all this is true, if that is the way we are, Frank, how could we build any kind of life on my betrayal, my abandonment, my sin?"

The bottle was half gone when I looked up and saw Virgil standing, blinking in the doorway.

"Hi, Virgil," I called. "When did you get back from Guatemala?"

He waved a hand and came to sit beside me.

"So you've fallen off the wagon, Frank?"

"No broken bones," I shrugged. "Will you have one with me?"

He shook his head and ordered a soft drink.

"Well?" he waited to hear my story, but his air of puritanical reproach aroused a perverse streak in me. I gestured airily.

"I've just been sitting here trying to work out a few problems," I said. "Have you ever noticed that life seems to be the resultant of a fluctuating tension between two poles. North pole, south pole: the positive and negative poles of a magnet, or even, let's say, the two poles that support the high wire of the tightrope walker."

He moved impatiently in his chair, but I fixed him with my glittering gaze.

"Let's play with analogies for a minute," I urged. "Let's imagine that each of us is the tightrope walker. Now, it's hard enough for any of us to get across that stretch of wire under the best of circumstances, but do you know what always happens to me, Virgil? Every time I climb up there and start off across the wire, one of my poles breaks."

165

"Come on, Frank." He started to rise, but I put a hand on his arm.

"Seriously, Virgil, that's my problem. They gave me an inferior set of equipment, and I don't know where to go to complain."

'I don't like to see you this way, Frank." he said, 'but I'm not going to scold you. We'd better get out of here right away. There's no telling what may happen."

I went over to say goodbye to the old lady and pressed one of my dwindling number of bills into her hand. Virgil had not been allowed to park Eduardo's car in the plaza itself, and we pushed through the crowd toward the corner where he had left it. The street mouth was blocked by soldiers.

"Nobody leaves the plaza," a swarthy corporal informed us."

"But there's our car parked right behind you," I argued. "We have nothing to do with all this."

"Those are my orders," he replied stolidly.

I swore and dragged Virgil with me across the plaza once more, through the milling throng to the command post in the mayor's office. The captain was too busy to see me, I was informed, and there were strict orders that no one was to leave the plaza.

"But why?" I protested.

The soldier — he was a sergeant this time — shrugged.

"They say General Calderón will be arriving in a little while to make a speech to everybody here," he answered.

"But we're foreigners," Virgil chimed in. "He's not interested in talking to us."

The sergeant shrugged again and turned away to talk to a messenger.

"Let's try one of the other streets," Virgil insisted. "I'd like to get away from here."

"It's all right," I soothed him. "The general is just going to scold these people and then send them home."

For the third time we pushed our way diagonally across the teeming square, this time to the corner nearest the *cantina*.

166

Virgil squared his shoulders and walked authoritatively up to the soldier nearest the wall.

"We have to get to our car," he said. "Please let us through."

The private hesitated, seemd about to give way, when the squad leader appeared at Virgil's side.

"You know your orders," he glared at the offender. "Nobody leaves until the general has finished."

We looked at each other helplessly, and Virgil shook his head. I remembered my half-empty bottle, and suddenly I was thirsty.

"Let's get out of the sun," I said craftily. "The last thing I want to do is stand here and listen to patriotic speeches."

Machiavellically, I led him to the *cantina*, debating whether I should stick with *aguardiente* or switch to beer.

"No, Frank!" He divined my intention and hung back. "You don't need any more to drink."

"You deeply wrong me, Virgil," I gave him a hurt look. "I have a plan to get us out of here."

The *cantina* was closed, the door locked. I knocked, and the old lady lifted a corner of the shade to squint at me apprehensively.

"Open up, grandma," I grinned at her. "Your best customer is back."

Still another soldier popped up at my side.

"It's closed," he told me. "All businesses on the plaza are closed."

I jerked my thumb toward the command post.

"But my friend, the captain, just asked me to bring him a cold bottle of beer. He said you'd let me in."

The soldier looked at me doubtfully, but I had a white skin and honest, blue eyes. I might have been a friend of the general himself. He nodded to the old lady, and she let us in.

I sank gratefully into a chair.

"You see?" I beamed at Virgil. "Isn't this better than broiling in the sun? A beer for me and a soft drink for my friend here," I added to grandma before Virgil could interpose a veto.

"Now tell me your plan," Virgil's tone was edged with distrust; he hadn't approved of my fib to the soldier.

"Phase one has been successfully accomplished," I assured him as the beer foamed up in my glass. "The next step is to wait until the general arrives and starts his speech. While his sturdy troops are gaping at him with awe and admiration, we will slip through the back door there, over the wall, and we will go tippy-toe down the street behind their backs."

My beer was almost gone, somehow. We heard the roar of truck motors outside.

"Here he comes." I raised my glass and polished off what was left in it. Virgil got up and went to the window, and I took advantage of his absence to wave frantically for another beer.

"I don't understand what's going on," Virgil said worriedly. "There are two trucks in front of the church, but it looks as though they're blocking all the streets with other trucks."

"It's been obvious all along that the general doesn't trust his oratorical ability alone to hold a crowd," I chuckled. I filled my glass rapidly and raised it to my lips.

At that instant we heard the first *raca-taca-taca* of the machine-guns.

"My God, Frank! It's an ambush!" Virgil blurted. "They're firing from the trucks!"

I overturned my chair getting to the window. A billow of shouts and screams muffled the next bursts of gunfire. The entire plaza was in violent motion: a mass of white costumes swirling like autumn leaves touched by a whirlwind.

The machine-guns were mounted on the truck beds, with army officers firing and feeding them. As we watched, the mass of peasants in the open, unprotected square recovered from the first shock, the first blind urge to escape. We watched the realization ripple through the agitated mass that there was no escape, that they were trapped. On the side opposite us, three or four figures appeared above the heads of

168

their comrades. They had been boosted off the ground and were scrabbling desperately for handholds on the edge of a low-lying roof. One actually gained the roof and was scuttling on hands and knees to safety when a machine-gun found him, sprawled him on the red tiles, then methodically stitched his dangling comrades against the walls to crumple and fall back to the ground.

"To the trucks! Take the trucks!" someone shouted close by our window. First a few, then a blind, screaming mass surged convulsively toward the muzzle of the machine-gun on the corner nearest us. They leaped over the bodies of the first victims. Some slipped in the blood on the paving stones; others pitched forward to writhe sluggishly as the bullets cut through them. I watched the machine-gunner on the truck across the square swivel his gun around to rake the charging mob, interpose an invisible wall that stopped them as effectively as stone and mortar, battered them to the ground in a nightmare of grotesque gestures, screams that bubbled and spewed blood, crimson stains that soaked and spread through inert white cloth. Despite the barrier of whispering death, a few got as far as the line of soldiers guarding the truck with fixed bayonets. They were spitted and thrown back to jerk spasmodically on the cobblestones.

"My God! My God!" Virgil's words were a mixture of expletive and prayer. I stood paralyzed, still unable to comprehend the meaning of what my eyes were recording. Fallen bodies formed an impassible tangle now, protecting the truck. The last group to attempt a charge was cut down as the barrier of bodies slowed it; its members fell on top of their dead and wounded companions. The screaming continued, but the note of surprise and rage was missing now. They were screams of sheer pain, pure agony.

A subtle change came over the mass of men in the plaza. They had stopped charging the trucks, and the insensate, milling movement slowed and stopped also, as if they had all simultaneously seized on the hope that some monstrous mistake had occurred; that if only they remained quiet, without moving, the machine-guns would be placated and would fall quiet too.

Virgil's bloodless hands gripped the window grating. We held our breaths, sharing the unvoiced hope. But the machine-guns kept on chattering; the bottles on the wall clinked against each other in response to the vibrations. The guns spoke in short, businesslike phrases now, methodically cleaning out the doorways, the edges of the plaza, like a tidy housewife sweeping dust out of the nooks and crannies to make a neat heap in the center of the floor.

A convulsion swept over the great, many-headed beast that lay agonizing under the sun, under the black funnel from Izalco boiling away to the east. The peasants herded together, crawling away from the steel-jacketed bees that ricocheted, whining, off the cobblestones around the edges of the square, scrabbling and clawing their way toward the middle of the open space, toward a temporary refuge behind the insubstantial wall of the still-living. They squirmed toward the center on their knees, on their bellies, and the machine-guns continued their terse, emotionless monologues, each one sweeping through its narrow angle of fire to avoid the other trucks and soldiers, each one searching out and stilling any signs of movement on the ground and then slicing neat chords through the edges of the living circle. The soldiers before the trucks had no employment for their bayonets now; they stood frozen, staring at the slaughter. The old lady had left the window and was wiping our table with steady, methodical strokes, while tears coursed down through her wrinkles.

All this had taken only a few minutes, I suppose. Most of the Indians huddled together in the center were still alive, still untouched or only slightly wounded. Even with half a dozen machine-guns it takes a long time to kill several thousand people.

Then, as the realization finally sank in that all this was actually happening out there before my eyes, as the full monstrosity and horror of it clutched my solar plexus — just then, Isabel, came the most incredible, the most unimaginable part.

Somebody in the huge, writhing huddle must have shouted something. I didn't hear him, but I suppose he must have shouted something like:

"If they're going to kill us, let's die standing up."

Or maybe he didn't shout it. Perhaps he only thought it as he rose to his feet, but his thought and his example communicated themselves like wildfire telepathy to other minds sensitized by the imminence of death.

The fact is that three or four men rose to their feet almost together. Then twenty...fifty...a hundred. They pushed themselves erect as if hypnotized, as if finally remembering something they had memorized years before, as children, but which they had forgotten for a long, long time.

Those who were standing, who had time to take a few steps, fumbled toward each other, formed an erratic, wavering column, and started walking slowly toward the church, toward the smoking muzzles of the two hysterical machine-guns that snarled at them from the trucks there. The front of the column crested and broke like a wave toppling on the sand. They fell as they walked: many of them, all of them, fell, writhed, and were still. Others got up to take their place, moving like sleepwalkers over and around the dead and wounded, walking quietly toward the two trucks.

"No!" Virgil sobbed. "No! No!" and he hurled himself at the door. I caught at his arm as he fumbled with the key, but he threw me across the room with a madman's strength.

"Virgil, don't be a damn fool!" I shouted, but he was gone.

It was as if he and I had also memorized our roles as children and had only remembered them now.

Virgil went out to the plaza. What did I do?

I went back to the window.

A middle-aged man and a boy of twelve or thirteen were getting to their feet, the boy gazing up at his father in terror and obedience.

171

"Get away from there!" the old lady shrieked at me as she locked the door again.

Virgil walked across to the two of them. He took the boy's other hand, and the three of them began walking toward the church. The old lady was standing beside me, staring with me out the window. I followed the three of them with my eyes until they fell...

Isabel:

I have returned Eduardo's car to his office. I have gathered some of Virgil's things (his Bible, his sermons, some shirts and clothing, his razor) and I have spent the night at his table, writing you. Why? To settle an outstanding account, perhaps — or to raise a candle to glimpse the face of truth. To tell you, in any event, that you were right.

     I love you,

       Frank

Chapter Eighteen

The shovel rythmically scatters the earth, the black, volcanic earth.

The ravens flutter about me, embrace me.

"She has gone to her reward," they caw at me. "You must be brave."

They are blotting out her face, and Neto's; Mamita Maria's, Papa Manuel's. Frank took with him one of her many faces, one he discovered in this patio, under this very light: one I never knew.

The earth keeps falling, covering her, covering them all. We leave her among the dead.

Related titles available from Curbstone Press

El Salvador:
LUISA IN REALITYLAND, a prose/verse novel by Claribel Alegría; trans. by Darwin J. Flakoll. A retrospect of the real, surreal and magical memories of childhood in El Salvador into which the realities of war gradually intrude. $9.95 pa./$17.95 cl.

ON THE FRONT LINE: Guerrilla Poems of El Salvador, edited & trans. by Claribel Alegría & Darwin J. Flakoll. A bilingual edition. More than poetry of combat, this volume is a record of the struggles, hopes and dreams of a war-torn country. $7.95pa.

MIGUEL MARMOL, by Roque Dalton; trans. by Richard Schaaf. Long considered a classic testimony throughout Latin America,*Miguel Marmol* gives a detailed account of Salvadoran history while telling the interesting and sometimeshumorous story of one man's life. $12.95pa./$19.95cl.

Nicaragua:
HAVE YOU SEEN A RED CURTAIN IN MY WEARY CHAMBER, selected writings by Tomás Borge; edited & trans. by Russell Bartley, Kent Johnson & Sylvia Yoneda. This first U.S. publication of Tomás Borge's poetry, essays and stories offers insight into this man, his work and the Nicaraguan Revolution. $9.95pa.

FLIGHTS OF VICTORY/VUELOS DE VICTORIA, poetry by Ernesto Cardenal edited & trans. by Marc Zimmerman, et al. In this bilingual edition, Cardenal celebrates his country's successful overthrow of the Somoza regime. Deeply religious and revolutionary, Cardenal's poetry is acclaimed throughout the world. $9.95pa.

Guatemala:
GRANDDAUGHTERS OF CORN: Portraits of Guatemalan Women by Marilyn Anderson & Jonathan Garlock. These photographs of Guatemalan women are accompanied by text that provides background for understanding the cultural as well as political realities in this turbulent country. $19.95pa./$35.00cl.

TESTIMONY: Death of a Guatemalan Village by Victor Montejo; trans. by Victor Perera. *Testimony* gives an eyewitness account by a Mayan school teacher of an army attack on a Guatemalan village and its aftermath, told in a clean and direct prose style. $8.95pa./$16.95cl.

FOR A COMPLETE CATALOG, SEND A REQUEST TO:
Curbstone Press, 321 Jackson St., Willimantic, CT 06226

ASHES
of
IZALCO

a novel by
CLARIBEL ALEGRIA
and
DARWIN J. FLAKOLL